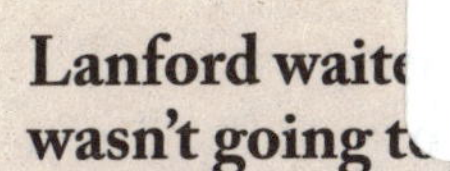

Lanford wait... wasn't going t...

Instead, Sarah sighed and uncrossed her arms to make a note on her list. “If I hear reports of you bothering people, I have to look into it.”

He nodded. He had his own plan. He needed to apologize and offer restitution to the people he’d hurt. If she heard that he was bothering someone, it might tell him who was still holding a grudge, which might be a lead to find the real killer.

He didn’t have a lot to work with.

“Anything else on your list of reasons for the crime?”

He almost relaxed. She’d accepted what he’d said, hadn’t tried to force him to share his information or refused to help him.

But remembering that last item he’d put on his list made his muscles tense, his heart rate speed up, a fight-or-flight reaction stepping in.

“I could have died.”

Her gaze shot to his, eyes widening. “Would someone still want to kill you?”

“I have no idea...”

Anne Galbraith grew up in the cold in Canada but now lives on a sailboat in the Caribbean, where she writes stories about happy-ever-afters. She enjoys sailing the blue waters, exploring new countries and sharing her characters with anyone who will read them. She's been a daughter, sister, wife, mother, teacher, accountant, and is now thrilled to add author to that list.

OUT OF THE ASHES

ANNE GALBRAITH

ISBN-13: 978-1-335-63340-8

Out of the Ashes

This edition published by arrangement with Harlequin Books S.A.

For questions and comments about the quality of this book, please contact us at CustomerService@Harlequin.com.

Love Inspired
22 Adelaide St. West, 40th Floor
Toronto, Ontario M5H 4E3, Canada
www.Harlequin.com

Printed in U.S.A.

Dearly beloved, avenge not yourselves,
but rather give place unto wrath: for it is written,
Vengeance is mine; I will repay, saith the Lord.

—*Romans* 12:19

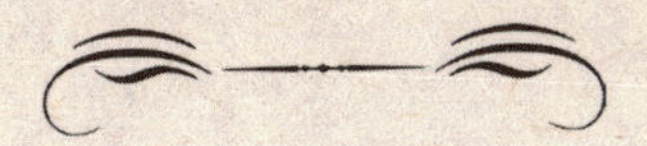

For Maggie K. Black, who helped me find this path.

And for Johanna, who inspired Festus.

Chapter One

She'd come to Balsam Grove to escape trouble, but it walked in her front door.

The front door of her police station, that is. Her police dog, Festus, promptly vanished under her desk.

"Trouble" in this case was six feet tall, with shaggy black hair, stubble and pale gray eyes. The man appeared to be about forty, not much older than she was. He was a stranger to her. After six months in town, she knew most of the residents, at least by sight. She'd never seen this man before.

Those eyes had a guarded, watchful expression. With his pale complexion and the faded, irregular tattoos on his knuckles, she identified him immediately as an ex-con. He stood stiffly, in new jeans and a T-shirt, showing he'd spent at least some of his time in prison working out.

Sarah Winfrey was a cop. She'd seen men like him before. She dropped her hand to her side, where it would be able to reach her weapon on her hip quickly. He hadn't made a threatening movement yet, but she didn't want to be caught unprepared. She had no idea why he was here.

At least he wasn't armed, based on what she could see from her position, seated at her desk.

But she wasn't a big-city cop anymore. She was the sheriff of a small town. And here in the sheriff's station, there was no bulletproof glass or protection. Just an exterior door leading to an open room that housed her desk, a seat for residents to come and make their complaints to her and a couple of chairs against the far wall.

He didn't sit.

He stood just inside the door and paused, giving her a look as assessing as the one she must be giving him. His eyes narrowed, his gaze scanning her features.

She wondered if he'd been able to categorize her as easily as she had him.

"You're the sheriff now?" His voice was rough. Smoker?

She nodded, waiting for him to explain why he'd come into her station.

"My name is Lanford Davies. I was sent to prison for the death of my family. Now I'm back. I've served my time, I'm sober and you'll see me at church. But I'm going to find whoever killed my family and sent me to prison for it. I won't cause trouble, but I want the truth. Thought I should let you know. I hope that won't be a problem for you."

With another look, he turned and walked back out the door of the station, leaving her speechless.

To date, Sarah's assignment in Balsam Grove had been a sinecure. Some lost hikers, or a drunk and disorderly on a Saturday night at the tavern. An occasional domestic, and teens drinking and vandalizing the school.

She'd taken this post for the quiet. She'd needed time to lick her wounds, regain her peace and sense of purpose. She wasn't expecting trouble.

But trouble had found her.

She waited, in case Lanford Davies returned, but the door stayed closed. A pickup drove by the window, followed by a couple of cars. The afternoon continued as usual for everyone else. Had that really happened?

She wrote down the name he'd given, Lanford Davies, on the pad of paper on her desk.

She hadn't come across anyone with the last name Davies in town. There were a few families out in the hills that she didn't know, but most of the people in town she recognized, at least by name.

She stood up to check the door. And barely saved herself from falling flat on her face.

She'd forgotten Festus.

Festus was the only other member of the sheriff's department. Or so she'd been told. She'd yet to find any way the dog would contribute to her job. She suspected Roy Harding, the previous sheriff, just hadn't wanted to take the dog with him to his retirement in Florida.

Presumably. He hadn't answered her emails or calls since she got here.

Festus, named for a deputy on a Western drama that had been a favorite of her predecessor's grandfather, was the least prepossessing police dog she'd ever seen. He was knee-high, partly brown, partly white, with bits of black scattered here and there. His ears perked up halfway and then drooped. He had a beer belly to rival that of the previous sheriff. His legs were just a little too short for his body, and his tail wagged up and down, rather than side to side.

He encompassed almost every breed of dog and, as a result, resembled none of them.

He would certainly be of no help in a crisis. When someone entered the building, such as Mr. Davies had, Festus would curl up under her desk and tremble.

If someone needed to be tripped, Festus might be able to assist. Beyond that, he was a mouth to feed and a body to walk. She was pretty sure that droopy middle of his had shrunk, a bit, under her regimen.

She was tempted to give herself points on her next self-review, for improvement in her detachment's physical conditioning.

Festus had one major redeeming quality. He was someone to talk to, since she spent most of her day alone.

"Thanks, Festus. Great help there."

Festus watched her, prepared to run for the file room in the back.

Sarah sighed. "Let's see if Mr. Davies is still around. I've got some questions."

She opened the front door and checked the sidewalk in each direction. No mysterious ex-con. No one walking this way. Festus stayed well back. She closed and locked the door.

She took a notepad and a pen and went into the back file room. It was located between the single holding cell and the kitchen and bathroom. Festus hovered at her heels.

One of the duties she'd assigned herself, since calls on her time weren't taxing, was to upload all the old paper records to the computer. She hadn't been in a rush, and she hadn't been searching for anything in particular.

Till now.

There weren't that many files, and if she couldn't find this one, she'd do some online research. She'd rather read the official records before the web mind influenced her with whatever conclusions it had come to.

Mr. Davies had admitted to being imprisoned. He hadn't explicitly said the crime that had sent him to prison had happened in Balsam Grove, but since he'd announced his intentions to her, she expected it had. It would behoove her to check into the case and get an idea what kind of problems he could bring to the town.

She wasn't sure exactly what trouble that was, but she could almost taste it.

She was familiar with guilty men maintaining their innocence. She'd arrested them. Testified against them. Prison was full of them. Not as many, once they were done their sentence and free to move on, set out to prove that innocence.

The odds were against Mr. Davies having been framed, even if there was a slight chance that he was right. She didn't expect he'd get far. But if he planned to delve into ancient history, she needed to be prepared.

The files in the back room were recorded by date, and she'd be looking for something within the past twenty-five years. Any further back and he would have been tried as a juvenile. Those records wouldn't be here.

She closed up the file cabinet she'd last digitized and turned to an older set of files.

"Come on, Festus. Let's see if we can find out what kind of trouble Mr. Davies is going to be."

* * *

Lanford returned to the church where he had been offered a place to stay. It was only two streets over from the police station. He'd left his duffel on the front step of the parsonage, since the minister hadn't been home when Lanford had first arrived in Balsam Grove. The pastor had posted a note for Lanford, saying that he'd return soon.

The minister was waiting for him now.

"You must be Lanford Davies." The smaller man held out his hand, and Lanford shook it. "I'm Harold Andrews. It's nice to meet you."

It had been a long time since anyone had considered it nice to meet Lanford.

"Thank you for what you're doing, Mr. Andrews."

"Call me Harold. May I call you Lanford?"

Lanford nodded.

"We built these two apartments for people who need assistance. Your prison chaplain went to seminary with me, so when he said you were looking for a place, I was happy to help. The place isn't much, but you're welcome to it."

Harold led him around the parsonage to a set of stairs at the rear.

The parsonage was a large, three-story brick building located beside the church. Long ago, when people had big families and servants, space such as this was necessary. Nowadays, the third floor was unused, so the church had made it into living quarters.

Lanford looked up the stairs to the two doors on the top landing. The apartment would be hot as summer came into force in another month or so, but Lanford wasn't complaining. It sure beat the cells he'd been sleeping in for the past eighteen years.

He followed Harold up the stairs.

"My wife put some linens in there, and there's some staples in the fridge and kitchen cupboards. It's furnished, not anything fancy, but it'll get you started."

Harold unlocked the door with a key that he then passed to Lanford and stood aside to let Lanford enter.

There was a couch and an easy chair. A TV. He didn't know if it was hooked up to anything. A tiny eating area and a small kitchen. There was a short hallway with two doors at the end.

"That's the bedroom and bathroom back there."

Lanford nodded, not moving far from the doorway.

"You're welcome to join our church services but it's not a requirement to stay here. We'd talked about you doing some work around the place, so come and see me about that, maybe tomorrow afternoon?"

Lanford nodded again. He wasn't used to talking much.

"I'll leave you to settle in. Let me know if you need anything."

He turned to Harold, hoping he hadn't appeared ungrateful. Lanford considered this an answer to prayer, one he'd not even put into words. He should say how much this meant to him.

"Harold…" Lanford paused. "I cannot tell you how much I appreciate this. You're an answer to prayer."

Harold's face lit up in a smile. "That's what I aim to be."

Lanford wasn't sure anyone would ever say that about an ex-con.

Harold left, leaving Lanford in his new home.

Home.

A temporary home. It wasn't easy to think of anything as permanent.

It was hard to accept that someone had that much faith in him, someone who didn't know him. He took it as a sign that God approved of his mission.

He didn't want revenge. Revenge would only lead him down a bad path. Lanford wanted justice.

This also gave him a purpose, in the short term, while he struggled to get his life together. To get some experience of life outside before he tried to imagine a future. He'd spent as many years of his existence in prison as not. It would take some adjustment. He needed to do it right because he had no intention of going back.

Lanford picked up the duffel bag and carried it into the bedroom. He took the few pieces of clothing he had and put them in the closet. He placed his razor, shampoo and body wash in the tiny bathroom. His well-worn Bible he set on the bedside table.

He pulled out the notebook and pens he'd purchased and went back to the main room. He sat down at the small table and opened the notebook.

He had a simple plan to find out the truth of that night, eighteen years ago. He'd had years to think it through, and he'd mentally prepared a list. He'd often heard *follow the money*. His family didn't have money. But he would follow the consequences of the events of that night.

He picked up a pen and clicked out the nib.

First consequence. *Dad died.*

His father was gone. Lanford hadn't spread the gas

or lit the match that had started the fire, but he feared he was responsible just the same.

His fingers were clenched tightly around the pen, and he deliberately loosened them. Lanford and his father had been on bad terms when the fire destroyed his world, and he would always regret that. He took a long breath.

Second consequence.

Riordan died.

His brother had been angry with him, as well. Lanford had been on course to mess up his life before the fire. Maybe prison had been a kind of blessing. He hadn't been able to hurt anyone else, and he'd finally found his peace. But someone had killed Dad and Dan, and that was not right.

Third consequence.

Property.

Their house, and the lot it was on, were the only assets the family had, the only thing someone might have coveted. The house had burned in the fire, but the property had still been of value. They'd lived just outside of town in a small house, set back in the trees. The lot wasn't any different from the others in the area, but there was no chance Dad would have sold it, not then. After the fire, it must have gone to someone. Not to him, obviously, since state law prohibited him from profiting from his crime. Maybe whoever had bought the land had needed it, badly enough to set a fire.

Fourth consequence.

I went to prison.

This was the most likely avenue to follow. He'd been nothing but trouble before the fire.

His mother had died when he was in grade school.

His dad had been on the road all the time, making deliveries as a long-distance trucker. Dan had been at college on a track scholarship, so Lanford had been home alone for long periods. Like a stupid kid, he'd gotten into trouble. It had been easy to find.

Parties, drinking, girls, shoplifting, joyriding, vandalism. He'd done it all. Lots of people would have been happy to have him gone.

Still, it was difficult to imagine anyone being so angry with him that they'd set fire to his house. Killing his father, his brother and almost Lanford himself.

He didn't remember a lot about that night. He'd been out partying before the fire.

Lanford had dragged himself home and passed out, drunk, on the couch. He'd been awakened by smoke, and stumbled his way out of the house, falling off the porch, rolling down the lawn and hitting his head on a rock.

When he came to, his house was an inferno. Beside him lay a jerry can, still with traces of gasoline in it. A lighter was stuffed in his pocket.

He hadn't set the fire. But no one believed him—not in court, not around town, not even his public defender.

One person knew the truth, though. One person knew, because that person had started the fire, not Lanford.

Lanford looked over his list of four consequences. One of these things may have inspired someone to burn down the house and set him up for the crime.

As he ran through the list, he realized there was one other outcome that could have happened that night. It chilled him to think of, but it was a possibility, so he should list it.

I could have been killed.

Maybe someone had hated him enough to want to kill him. If that person was still in town, would time have changed that hatred? Someone could still want him dead.

Chapter Two

Sarah didn't head to the station first thing the next morning.

Once she'd dragged Festus out of bed for a half-hour walk, she'd shoved him in the police vehicle and followed the GPS directions to the former Davies property.

Yesterday she'd found the Davies file and read it through. She was anxious to find Lanford Davies and talk to him, but the only address in the file was the house that had been burned down in the arson.

She could reach out to the probation office to get the address he'd provided them with, but probation officers were sometimes territorial, and it might take a while to find where Mr. Davies was residing and if there were any special probation terms she needed to be aware of. Something it would have been nice to have been notified of. As well, she didn't want to cause any problems for Mr. Davies, in case he was actually trying to keep clean and out of trouble.

Balsam Grove was a small town. Sarah would definitely recognize Davies if she saw him again. She'd try the happenstance approach before she went through official channels.

But she was curious. The case was circumstantial, and she had a strong drive to find the truth, not just what was convenient. Her father had been a detective. He'd raised her on stories of his cases instead of fairy tales. For him there was right and wrong, truth and lies, and he had a passion for justice. She'd always wanted to be the same. She wouldn't dismiss out of hand the possibility of a false arrest and sentence. There had been no witnesses. But no one else had been found near the scene, and there was no apparent motive.

She hadn't had to exercise any detective muscles since she'd arrived here in Balsam Grove. This could be interesting.

"Festus, we're going to check out the scene of the crime. This is your chance to awe and amaze me, okay?"

She needed to get out more. She was spending too much time talking to her deputy.

"Don't worry, after eighteen years, it's unlikely either of us will find any missed clues, but nothing ventured, nothing gained, right?"

Festus curled his tail around his nose, hidden in the passenger footwell.

"Glad you've got it under control."

The address wasn't far out of town. She could have easily walked. Festus? Not so much.

When her GPS said the destination was on her right, she had two reasons for surprise.

First, she hadn't realized that this address was the U-Stor storage facility. It was part of the town landscape now, but apparently it was less than eighteen years old.

Secondly, the man she'd been hoping to find was standing on the driveway, peering through the fence.

She pulled her vehicle to the side and braked. She switched off the SUV and paused for a moment, watching the man.

He shot her a glance, then continued with his own quiet inspection.

Again, he was in a T-shirt and jeans. He must have walked: there was no other mode of transportation apparent. No sign of a weapon, which would have been a violation of his parole.

She opened her door and left the vehicle. She crossed to let Festus out, and he slunk to the ground. With a quick glance to make sure Festus wasn't likely to wander onto the road, she walked over to Mr. Davies.

"Good morning, Mr. Davies. I'm happy to run into you."

He paused for a moment and then turned to face her. "You found me."

She nodded at the building behind them. "Did you know your home had been made into a storage facility?"

He frowned. "No, Sheriff. I didn't."

He gazed at his feet. "Any other questions?"

She drew in a breath.

"That may have sounded like I was interrogating you, but it was just nosiness on my part. I can only imagine that coming back to find this, if you didn't expect it, would be...jarring."

His glance came up to meet hers again. Those gray eyes narrowed as he looked at her, perhaps adjusting his opinion. For some reason, she hoped it was changing to something better.

No, no, no. She was not getting involved here. Not

again. She needed to prove that she was more like her father, not her grandfather. She'd walked too close to that line on the last case in Pittsburgh.

Even with the rough-cut hair and the pale complexion, Lanford Davies was an attractive man.

She could not afford to lose her objectivity again. Not if she was returning to the city.

"I wondered what had happened to the place." He glanced over at the boxy building. "Now I know."

She tilted her head, trying to interpret his tone.

It didn't have the anger in it that she'd expect of someone thirsting for revenge. There was no greed, since he couldn't profit from his crime.

He'd said he was here to prove his innocence. Did he have someone in mind, someone he believed had done this to him? What did he plan to do about it? Even if he only wanted to clear his name, he'd have to take some kind of action.

And that action could involve her, in her role as sheriff.

"I looked up your file last night, Mr. Davies."

He nodded.

"I'd like to ask you some questions."

She saw his shoulders tighten, his neck brace. She had the authority to force him to come to the station, even if morally she was less complacent. She didn't want him to talk to her, every word forced out, begrudging and unwilling, simply because she was a cop and he'd been in prison.

He didn't have any reason to trust her, just as she didn't have reason to trust him. However, they could both help each other and possibly circumvent problems if they worked together.

She just had to convince him of that.

"I'm the sheriff, but I'm not going to force you to talk to me.

"You told me you want to prove your innocence. I have an interest in ensuring justice is done. I also have an interest in being aware of what steps you're taking—in case something blows up, so I don't have to come into whatever that situation is blind.

"I can help you look into what happened eighteen years ago. I wasn't here, and I have limited preconceptions of what happened and who was involved."

She checked his expression, but it was just as guarded as it had been yesterday.

"I don't know if you're innocent. But I *want* to know. I would prefer if you talked to me willingly and gave me some insight into what might be going on in my jurisdiction while you're here. You can ask me questions, and perhaps we could work together.

"No pressure. I'm just offering."

She stepped away, hands in her back pockets, purposely giving him space.

And time.

"Why would you want to upset a conviction that happened eighteen years ago? It's not going to make you or Sheriff Harding look good. It's going to be a lot of hassle and paperwork."

It would—he was right.

"Mr. Davies, I came here from Pittsburgh. I had my reasons, but so far this position has been kind of boring. I became a cop because I wanted to be one of the good guys, and to help people who needed justice on their side. I enjoy investigating. I like putting evidence together and making sure the bad guys pay.

"If you were innocent, then it would be worth any hassle or paperwork in my estimation. That's how I was raised. And reexamining your case would give me some interesting work to do."

He watched her, trying to read beyond her words. She was sincere, but he couldn't know that. She hoped he'd give her a chance. And that she wasn't crossing the line that had gotten her into trouble before.

Sometimes her sense of right and wrong didn't align with that of her fellow police officers. Her grandfather had crossed that line so badly that the line had been lost, and her father had worked hard to redeem the family reputation. She wanted to make her father proud, and that last case had…

Well, it had caused a few people to question her motives. She would have to watch that here, as well.

But underneath, she still wanted to make sure the truth came out.

He nodded as he came to a conclusion. She wasn't sure what had inspired him to make his decision, but she was sure it was more than the words she'd said.

"I would be willing to discuss it with you. I'm not making any promises."

"I'm not asking you to. Not right now."

Depending on what he had in mind, that could change.

She turned to her car, and he followed her.

"Want a ride to the station? So we can get started?"

"I can walk."

She took a moment to consider if there was a reason for that, beyond wanting exercise and to enjoy the freedom of going where he wanted after eighteen years locked up.

"Or you can ride beside me in the passenger seat. I have no intention of putting you in the back, as if I was arresting you."

He shot her a glance.

"Okay." Again, she had the impression that he was evaluating the situation at a level several steps beyond the superficial conversation they were having.

"Festus!"

The dog came around the SUV, spotted Lanford Davies and promptly tried to crawl under the vehicle.

She could extrapolate from the dog's actions that he'd found the man beside her lacking. That he had some special dog sense that could detect flaws in human character. But for the first week she'd been in town, Festus had reacted the same way to her. He was no lodestar, divining between good and evil.

"That's your dog?"

"He's part of the sheriff's department."

Mr. Davies snorted in disbelief.

"Tell me about it." She got down on her knees to coax the dog out.

Lanford wasn't sure what to make of this sheriff.

He was skeptical of the police after what he'd been through. When they'd arrested him, he'd told everyone that he was innocent, but no one had been willing to listen. He'd been the easy solution to the problem of who had set fire to his house.

In prison, he'd heard stories from men who'd had difficult interactions with the police. Men who'd been sent back to prison after getting out and dealing with the stigma of having a record. It made them immediately suspect.

If he hadn't been determined to stay out of prison and avoid any difficult interactions with local law enforcement in Balsam Grove, he'd have stayed as far away from the sheriff's office as possible.

It had been a relief to find someone new behind the desk. At least she wouldn't have memories of him telling her off when he was a mouthy kid. He'd never given her the finger or told her where to go. But she was still a cop, and there was a big gap between her and an ex-con. He wasn't naive now. She might only be pretending to want to help. He'd experienced the other side of law enforcement. Caution was required.

She hadn't immediately accepted his story, which would have been suspicious in any case. But she was allowing for the possibility that he was innocent. Maybe.

She wanted to know what he was doing.

He couldn't suspect she was in collusion with the real arsonist because he had no idea who that was, and she wouldn't know him or her. Her reason for wanting to be involved made sense. If she was truly willing to assist him in finding the truth, it would be a lot of help. As long as she *did* want to uncover the truth and wasn't just saying that to be in a position to cover it up later.

He'd never ridden in the front seat of a police car. It was much better than the rear seat. In his recollection, that had been smelly, claustrophobic, and his sorrow and shock had seeped into the memories in his mind.

He glanced over his shoulder at the supposed police dog. The dog was cowering in the far corner of the back seat, but somehow still giving him the stink eye.

What in the world was she doing with a dog like that?

She and Lanford didn't speak on the way to the sheriff's department. Lanford was considering and reconsidering his decision to share with her. She appeared lost in her own thoughts, as well.

When they pulled in behind the station, he got out of the SUV and waited for her to exit. It took a few moments to persuade Festus out of the back seat. Lanford had no idea how such a fearful animal was claimed by the law office.

The sheriff didn't seem to be that fond of him, either, which made it more of a puzzle. But not his. He had enough to figure out already.

She opened the door, and Festus fled into the interior. Lanford followed her into the building. She flipped on the lights and unlocked the front door. He stood, unsure of where to go while she checked for voice mails.

There were none.

The sheriff picked up a thick file. His name was on it. She crossed to a small table and pulled out a chair.

"I thought we could work through the case here."

He nodded and crossed to the seat opposite her, pulling it out and sitting down. This wasn't a commitment. He could still decide how much he was willing to tell her.

She had a pad of paper and a pen. He had nothing. His notebook was still at the apartment.

"What's your plan?" she asked, without any expression of skepticism. "Who do you think set you up?"

Lanford shook his head. "I have no idea."

She considered for a moment.

"You have someplace you want to start?"

He nodded.

The sheriff waited, letting him decide what he wanted to share with her.

He took a breath. He'd prayed about this. She wasn't

raising any red flags. What he had to share wasn't a secret.

"There's an expression, follow the money. That's where I'm starting."

She frowned. "I read your file. I didn't find any indications of much financial gain from what happened."

He clenched his fists. He wasn't explaining this properly.

"Not actual money. But what happened, what the results were."

Her eyes widened as she understood his point. "Explore the consequences and find out who benefited."

"Yes."

She started to write on her pad of paper, but then paused.

"What are those consequences?"

Lanford brought his list to mind.

"My dad died." He stopped short. He couldn't force words out through his throat, which had closed up.

The pain still survived from that horrible night. After eighteen years, he'd come to terms with it. It didn't normally gut him. But sometimes it stabbed through him as if he'd received the news fresh. His dad was dead. He hadn't spread the gas or lit the match, but he was afraid he was responsible just the same.

She wrote something down.

"Who benefited from that?"

"I don't know." If he did, he would have names to explore.

She tilted her head, questioning him. "Then what can you do?"

"I'm going to talk to the company he worked for."

"He was a long-distance trucker, right?"

"That's right."

The sheriff tapped her pen. "What about his personal life?"

"None."

She leaned back in her chair.

"As a teenager, you might not have been aware of things that went on in your father's personal life."

He half smiled. "I understand what you're implying. I'm not naive. Not anymore."

Eighteen years in prison was a crash course in learning what people were capable of.

"My mother died of cancer, and my dad was devastated. He had no personal life. He worked, and he took care of us. That was it."

He could see the skepticism on her face. That wasn't her decision, though. This was his investigation. He didn't need to work with her.

"I'm not going to waste time looking into nothing."

She made another note. Maybe she wanted to ask around about his dad's personal life. She was welcome to. She wouldn't find anything.

"Is there any chance he might have been hauling something illegal or dangerous?"

"Not that he would have done knowingly."

Lanford had no doubts about that. He wasn't going to waste his efforts on that, either.

"Then why would anyone wish him harm?"

"Someone might have wanted his job, his routes." It was the only thing he'd come up with after mulling it over for years.

She exhaled. "Okay. What else happened?"

"Dan died."

Her forehead creased. "Oh, you mean Riordan. Your brother."

He nodded. He hadn't been able to say Riordan when he was little, so they'd been known as Dan and Lan.

"What were the consequences of that?"

"Dan had a scholarship, for track. Maybe another kid or his family wanted it."

Lanford didn't know much about his brother's life at school. Dan was a straight-arrow kind of guy, so it was hard to imagine he'd gotten into anything that would endanger his life, or that of the rest of his family, but again, there were limited trails to follow.

She was writing again.

"Penn State, right?"

He nodded again. It had been a big day at their home when Dan got that news.

"I worked with someone, in the city. He must have been at Penn about that time. He was a football player. I'll ask him to check into the athletic department, see if there was anything talked about concerning your brother."

Lanford thought he had a good chance at getting his dad's former boss to speak with him. When he was a kid, he'd met the man at company events. But the university? He had no idea how to explore that.

This sheriff might be a help. If he could trust her. If she wasn't doing this to cut off any chance he had of getting the information he was searching for.

Was there any reason not to let her speak to her co-worker about Dan?

He studied her face, doing his best to read her expression and understand what she wanted out of this. All he could find was intelligence and concern.

And honestly, there was nothing he could do to stop her. But his control over the investigation was slipping away from him, and he wasn't sure that was good.

"Okay. Thank you."

She smiled. "What else?"

"The property."

"Now a storage facility. Do you know how that happened?"

He shook his head. "I have no idea. I was more worried about going to prison and what was going to happen to me than the land."

"That's understandable. Let's find out."

His fists clenched. Who was in control here? If it wasn't him, how could he be sure he'd find the truth?

The sheriff let her hands fall into her lap.

"You've opened Pandora's box, Mr. Davies. If you tell me someone has committed murder and gotten away with it, I'm going to investigate it. Especially now, when I'm not busy with other things. I need to know if a killer is still in Balsam Grove, walking around, believing he or she has gotten away with it, and perhaps willing to do something similar again in the right circumstances."

He couldn't stop her. And it was in his best interests to be kept in the loop if she learned something.

He nodded, hoping he hadn't made a mistake.

Chapter Three

Sarah's fingers were tingling. She hadn't had any serious detective work to do in months, and she couldn't wait to use her intelligence and her training in the way she loved.

The first steps were simple. She used the computer to track the property in the county system.

"This property passed to a cousin of your father's in Australia after your trial and probate. A month later, a holding company bought it. U-Stor opened two years after your arrest." She didn't need to date it from his family's deaths. That would be cruel.

He nodded.

It was easy to guess that the cousin had been happy to sell the property located halfway around the world. The cousin, using the term loosely, had been eighty years old, so unlikely to travel to the US for a piece of rural property. It was equally difficult to imagine him traveling to Balsam Grove and setting a fire.

But the transfer to the holding company had followed within a month of the deed passing to the cousin. That was quick. She'd look further into that.

She picked up her smartphone and did an online search for the storage company.

A lot of storage facilities were chains, and most were built in larger towns and cities where there was a larger base of potential customers, as well as smaller homes and apartments with less internal storage.

U-Stor was the only facility owned by its parent company. U-Stor's website was small and amateurish. It didn't look like it had been updated recently. The structure of the storage facility was simple, so the construction period probably hadn't been long, but someone had obviously been eager to build the place.

Lanford waited quietly while she researched.

"Was there another storage place here, do you remember?"

Lanford shook his head.

She twisted her lips. "Maybe you wouldn't have known about it."

A barking sound from Lanford. It was a laugh, of sorts. She blinked, surprised.

"If there'd been anything like that around, my friends and I would have known."

"Why's that?" Perhaps it was some kind of rural thing. Growing up in the city she hadn't been especially aware of any storage facilities.

"We were always looking for places we could get in trouble. A storage building would have been perfect."

Sarah studied the man across from her.

"Yeah, I got in trouble. A lot."

His body had gone rigid, and his fists had clenched. This had been an argument against him at his trial.

"A lot of teenagers get in trouble. That doesn't mean they're arsonists."

He didn't relax. His brow furrowed as he watched her.

"You believe me?"

She wasn't going to lie. Her moral compass was firm on "Thou shalt not bear false witness" and "Let your communication be, Yea, yea; Nay, nay."

"I'm not sure yet, Mr. Davies. I don't know you, and I've barely had time to review your file."

He relaxed when she said that, which surprised her.

"That doesn't upset you?"

"I can handle honest. I don't care for people who say one thing, mean another."

"I don't, either. I will be as honest with you as I can."

The eyes staring back at her were wary, but she also saw intelligence there. She wondered what he'd done with himself in prison. He couldn't have caused too much trouble, since he'd been released early. Had he studied law? Gotten a degree?

"What might cause you to not be honest?" He was interested in her response, unsurprisingly.

"I won't lie. But I may not be able to tell you something you want to know. I'm an officer of the law, not your private investigator."

His head cocked. "But you're still checking into this? My claims to be innocent?"

She nodded. "That doesn't conflict with my job. The opposite, in fact."

As her father had taught her. This time, he nodded. As if he'd accepted something about her.

"So..." She continued with her previous chain of

thought. "There wasn't a storage facility here before. It might just be a coincidence that your family's land was available. Do you know if people in town needed local storage? Did they have to travel to find it?"

He shook his head. "My family didn't store anything except at our place. We had room. So do most of the folks around here. We wouldn't have paid to put it somewhere else."

"Good point. Let's find out how busy they are at U-Stor."

Sarah reopened the website on her phone and hit the call icon. She held a finger to her lips and then hit the hands-free option.

After three rings, a female voice answered. "U-Stor, here for all your storage needs. How can I help you?"

"Well, y'all can help me if you have some space there. And I mean, a lot of space."

She saw Lanford blinking, surprised by the Southern drawl coming out of her mouth. Her mother was from Georgia, and Sarah had heard that way of speaking all her life. It was her party trick: she could sound like she was from the South with the flick of an internal switch.

"We do have some openings. How much stuff do you need to put in storage?"

"I'm not sure exactly, not yet. My husband's aunt broke her hip, and she just can't stay living on her own. We have got to get her into a home. But she's a hoarder. You know, just like on those TV shows? And she's having a conniption about her stuff. My husband promised her we'd put everything in storage, so she can look at it later. We're hoping we can put her off and just throw everything out after a bit, but if we're gonna get her out of that house without a fight, she has to know her stuff is going somewhere.

"We haven't been to her place for a couple of years, but the house was full, and I think the garage is, too. We might need a *lot* of storage.

"If you don't have the space, we can find somewhere else, but so far you're the closest place that might have room."

"Oh, we do—have room, that is." The woman's voice lowered. "Just between you and I, this place isn't very full, so we have tons of room. Most of the biggest lockers, as well as half of the smaller ones."

"Oh, that is such a relief. Let me grab my pen so you can give me your rates, okay?"

After a moment, Sarah continued. "I'm ready."

The woman on the phone started to rattle off sizes and dollar amounts. Sarah said "uh-huh" and "got that" but didn't write down any of the information.

"We're heading up next week—are you sure you'll still have the space then?"

"Oh, yes, ma'am, it's really not busy here. Did you want to leave a deposit?"

"Let me get— Oh, Fido, get off there. Fido! I'm sorry, I've got to go before that dog digs up my azaleas!"

She tapped the disconnect button. The dog, who'd heard the yelling, crawled around behind her chair and slithered into the file room.

Sarah sighed, then turned to Lanford Davies.

"Your property was purchased almost as soon as possible, to build a storage facility that appears unnecessary and unprofitable. Maybe I'm leaping to conclusions, but that makes me wonder if there's something to investigate."

* * *

Lanford turned from watching the sorriest excuse for a police dog he'd ever seen slipping away into a back room and focused on the current law in Balsam Grove.

He'd been surprised when he found a woman manning the sheriff's station. He probably shouldn't have been, but there'd never been a female law officer in Balsam Grove that he'd heard of. Times had moved on while he was in prison.

He'd also been surprised to find her at his former home this morning. He'd assumed she'd write him off as a crackpot and leave him be. He'd hoped she wouldn't work against him. He hadn't expected that she'd work *with* him.

She didn't believe him, not yet, but she was willing to be convinced. That was the biggest surprise.

His experiences with law enforcement hadn't been positive. When he'd been getting in trouble as a teenager, he'd been on the opposing side, though he could now appreciate that was mostly his fault. Being sentenced for a crime he was innocent of hadn't made his view any more positive.

Prison had reinforced that division.

If she was willing to entertain the possibility that he could be innocent, he should probably do the same for her. Maybe she was a good cop.

Not that he'd share everything with her.

"You think it's suspicious because the storage place is empty?"

She nodded.

"Any kind of businessperson opening up a new enterprise like this storage facility would do research. If there isn't enough demand for their product, it sounds like they didn't do proper due diligence. Especially when they bought the place so quickly."

"You think they burnt our house so they could build a storage place?"

She shook her head. "No, it's not your property that has value, Mr. Davies."

"Call me Lanford."

He hadn't planned to say that. But he didn't want her calling him *Mr. Davies. Mr. Davies* sounded formal, old. It implied a respect he hadn't deserved or mockery that didn't sit well with him.

"Unless someone is playing a very long game and there's a hidden oil reserve under your land, it seems odd that it sold so quickly. There was a lot near yours that was sold about the time I moved here: the real estate agent showed it to me when I was looking for a place. It took a while to sell. No one has been buying up land around your family's place over the last eighteen years, so I doubt someone committed a crime just to get the land."

That made sense.

"Another option would be acquiring the land to keep something hidden. But your father wasn't planning to sell or build anything, right?"

"Not that I heard of."

"And building that storage facility means that the whole place was pretty well dug up. Nothing was hidden that would have been exposed otherwise.

"I'll do some more research, but I have to wonder if there was a financially sound reason to build a storage facility on your land. Maybe it's nothing to do with your case, and it could be connected to something else of interest to me like money laundering, but I'm going to check who owns the company, and if they've got more holdings."

He'd never considered anything like that. He'd put the sale of the property down just because he was being thorough. His dad hadn't planned to sell the place, but why would anyone want their lot more than any other?

No reason he could come up with.

"Do you think this supports my story?" They'd basically proven that no one had wanted the property.

"It's possible. Maybe the owner is just a poor businessperson, but spite is also an option. I can look into the person behind the corporation, find out who it is. If I give you some names, can you tell me if any of them would have had ill will toward you or your family?"

He drew a long breath. Might as well get it out there. She had those police files; she'd find this out anyway.

"That's possibility number four."

"You mean someone did this to get back at you, personally."

He nodded.

Her expression had changed. When they were talking about the storage place, her face had relaxed. She'd been open, even a little excited. She'd wanted to solve this puzzle.

Now her features were stiff, set in what he called a cop face. No expression, nothing given away.

He was surprised how much that bothered him.

He'd started to…like her. She'd been willing to talk to him, to help. He'd never thought he'd have an ally on this journey. She had access to resources he couldn't touch.

That could end—now. And she could shut down his chances of succeeding on his own, as well.

"I got in a lot of trouble, as I mentioned. There were people who didn't care for me." People like the former sheriff, Roy Harding. Lanford had been picked up for a bunch of stupid stuff: vandalism, shoplifting, drinking underage. And he'd been mouthy, disrespectful to the sheriff and others.

"Who would that person or persons be?"

"It's a long list. I appreciate the help you've offered, but this consequence is mine to explore."

She crossed her arms, cop face still on. He'd probably cost himself her help, and he regretted that.

But he couldn't very well tell her everyone in town had been glad to see him gone.

But another reason kept him quiet. This woman didn't know the boy he'd been. The people he'd hurt, the property he'd damaged, the stupid things he'd done. It shouldn't bother him that she'd find out. He was an ex-con; it wasn't likely that he'd fall in her estimation.

Still, he didn't want to list all the stupid, mean, petty things he'd done.

He waited for her to say she wasn't going to help him. He braced himself, realizing he wasn't done with all his stupid behavior.

Instead, she sighed and uncrossed her arms to make a note on her list.

"If I hear reports of you bothering people because of your investigation, I have to check into it."

He nodded. He had his own plan. He needed to apologize and offer restitution to the people he'd hurt. If she heard that he was bothering someone, it might tell him who still held a grudge, which might be a lead.

He didn't have a lot to work with.

"Anything else on your list?"

He almost relaxed. She'd accepted what he'd said, hadn't tried to force him to share his information, or refused to help him.

But remembering that last item he'd put on his list made his muscles tense, his heart rate speed up, a flight-or-fight reaction stepping in.

"I could have died."

Her gaze shot to his, eyes widening.

"Would someone still want to kill you?"

"I have no idea."

Chapter Four

Sarah offered to drive Lanford back to where he was staying.

"That's okay. It's not a long walk."

She tapped her pencil. She was still a little shaken from his last consequence.

When the job for sheriff of Balsam Grove had been posted, detective skills in homicide and arson had not been listed as requirements. Yes, she had access to the state police, but she'd never expected that a murder was likely to happen here.

She wasn't sure of Lanford. Part of her was ready to give him the benefit of the doubt. Part of her wondered if she was being played.

His refusal to talk about who might have wanted him arrested didn't encourage her to trust him.

She hadn't pushed because she could find out that information on her own. Juvie records were sealed, but it was a small town. Her neighbor had already been ready to share the town gossip with her, and since Arthur was newly retired and a lifelong resident, he'd be familiar with the story of Lanford Davies.

If someone out there might want to finish the job he or she had started eighteen years ago and obliterate the last member of the Davies family, she needed to keep an eye on Lanford. Offering him a ride home had been a way to track his location without asking directly. She didn't want to freak him out. But if he was in danger, it was her job to protect him.

She'd have to get ahold of his probation officer, find out his address. If he was going to stay on the straight and narrow, he'd have filed an address with them, and it would be a real one.

At least she had work to do for the next while.

Lanford stood up to leave, so she stood, as well.

"I appreciate your help," he said.

She glanced down at her notes. "I'll reach out to my guy from Penn State and in the meantime do some digging into U-Stor."

He tilted his head.

"You're still going to help me?"

She put her hands on her hips. "I'm going to do my job. If you didn't set that fire, someone else did, and killed two people. I'm opposed to criminals getting away with murder."

"Thank you." There he was, acting innocent again. "I'm staying at the parsonage, the Second Street church. The pastor offered me a place to stay and some work to do."

"Good to know. Do you have a phone? Mobile or landline?"

He shook his head. "Not yet. Things are a little different from before I went in. I'll inform you once I have a number. Goodbye, Sheriff."

He turned and left. Sarah stared after him, trying to figure him out.

Festus came out of the file room, eyeing the empty space suspiciously.

"Cheer up, wonder dog. You're still safe."

Festus trudged over to his water bowl and started lapping. Sarah returned to her desk.

She checked over her list.

Five reasons someone might have poured gasoline, lit a match and killed two people before putting the gas can and lighter by Lanford.

Unless Lanford had done it himself.

The most innocuous reason, a desire to acquire the family property, was one she could research. She'd dig into the ownership of that corporation, how they acquired the land from the cousin, and how much was paid.

She hoped Lanford wouldn't be as evasive about anything she found from that as he had been with consequence number four. Because she was not his personal information department. She was going to investigate this, and she'd find out the truth if at all possible. She would do it with or without Lanford Davies's cooperation.

If he didn't help, then she wasn't going to share her information with him.

She checked her phone messages, making sure there were no other demands on her time currently. She made note of two calls that had come in, neither of them urgent.

Then she scrolled through her contacts to find Chad, her former coworker, who had loved to talk about his days playing football at Penn State.

She left a message on his phone, not surprised that he was too busy to answer right away. Then she started to research U-Stor.

It was owned by a numbered corporation. That wasn't necessarily sketchy. People often left a corporation name as a number, since coming up with a creative, appropriate name that wasn't already claimed could be a problem. And sometimes people were just lazy.

And then, other times, they were hiding.

Her cell phone rang.

"Hey, Chad, thanks for returning my call."

"You're still alive!"

Sarah snorted. "Living outside of a city isn't a death sentence, Chad. At least, not yet."

"Maybe so, but I'm not taking that chance. Do they even have a Starbucks?"

"No, but they have a diner. Coffee is good there."

"Coffee, sure, but what about a macchiato?"

Sarah shook her head. "No, they don't have that. Guess you're not going to transfer here anytime soon."

"No can do, Sarah. How are things going out there?"

He made it sound as if she'd crossed half the country in a wagon train.

"Quiet. Really quiet."

"Ah, sorry about that, Sarah. You can return here, you know. You left on your own."

Sarah was quiet for a moment. She'd left for a reason. She wasn't sure if she was ready to go back, or if she wanted to. If she was wanted and trusted. Dealing with Lanford Davies would distract her for a while, maybe give her space to decide if she was ready to return.

"Thanks, Chad, but I did come up with a little problem here, something to keep me busy."

"That's good. But don't forget you belong here."

She cocked her head. "Let me guess, the new guy isn't a good bowler."

A pause, then Chad responded. "It's not *just* that. I promise."

Sarah laughed. "At least I have a secret weapon if I want to work my way back onto the squad."

"You don't need a secret weapon, Sarah. You're a good cop."

She *was* a good cop. There had just been a little confusion as to the definition of the term good in respect to being a cop. Her grandfather had been a dirty cop, and her father had struggled all his life to fight to prove he wasn't the same. Sarah had made some of her fellow officers wonder if she was more like her grandfather than her dad.

At the time, she'd believed her actions justified, but until she sorted out where her definitions fit, she was probably better off staying here. She had half a year left on her leave.

"Can you give me a bit of help on that problem I mentioned?"

"Sure." She could hear the surprise in Chad's voice. "Something you can't do through regular channels?"

"This requires some insider knowledge of the athletic department at Penn State."

There was a pregnant pause. Sarah belatedly remembered there'd been a scandal in the football department.

"Not what you're thinking, Chad. This is about a kid running track from eighteen years ago. He died in a fire, arson."

"Okay, Sarah. Why do you care about something from those days?"

"A dad and this kid, a college runner at Penn, died in a fire. The brother was found guilty of setting the fire, third-degree murder. He's served his time, just got out and is on the search for the person he says really did it."

"Another innocent one?" Sarah heard the skepticism in his voice.

"That was my first response, too. But they don't usually try to prove it after they get out."

"Unless they're hoping for a settlement. This got a DNA angle?"

"Nothing in the file referencing that. The case was circumstantial, but no other suspects. Still, the guy is here in town, going to dig around, and I want to keep on top of it. I hoped you might have some contacts that could tell me if this young man who died had a reason someone might want to kill him."

"I could probably find someone, yeah, but are you sure this is a good idea?"

She understood he was asking from a place of caring, but it still bothered her.

"I've got time on my hands, and in case something ugly gets dug up, I'd rather be ahead of the game, not reacting."

She heard Chad chewing—he used gum to keep himself from smoking.

"Yeah, I have a couple of guys I could call. What's this kid's name?"

"Riordan Davies. His nickname was Dan. He ran the 400, had a full ride, so I assume he was good. Maybe he was good enough that someone wanted to get rid of him?"

She heard Chad sigh through his gum. "I'd like to say that doesn't sound feasible, but we both know it's a strange world. I'll get the scoop on the track situation from, when again?"

"Eighteen years ago. Riordan had just completed his sophomore year. I thought that put him near your days at Penn."

"I graduated nineteen years ago, so not much of an overlap, but I'll ask around."

"Thanks, Chad. If there's anything I can do for you…"

Sarah expected a quick rebuttal. She couldn't imagine Chad needing information she had on this small town.

"Sarah—you're sure you're not getting too involved?"

Sarah hissed in a breath. Anger sparked. She wanted to tell Chad what to do with that question.

She couldn't, though. She'd gotten too involved before, and that was why she was here, bored with a job that didn't challenge her.

She did get involved. She cared. That wasn't a bad thing. But there was a line where the job, the long-term good, had to take priority over the immediate. Where helping a person might depend on who that person was.

She had set that line in a different place than the rest of her team, and that had messed up an operation. Before she went back to the city, she had to be sure she could rearrange her line to match the others'.

Otherwise, they'd never trust her. There'd be no point in returning.

So instead of yelling, she assured Chad she wasn't too involved.

"I'm good, Chad. But now that we're asking questions that someone might not want asked, we could stir up trouble."

Chad's voice was more relaxed now that he had his question settled.

"You're right. We don't often have time to prepare for things we see coming. You take care."

Festus rolled over on Sarah's foot.

She was more likely to fall over the dog than need to take any other precautions.

"Don't worry—my biggest hazard is the police dog. You take care, too, and thanks for doing this for me."

"No problem. But let me know how it works out. I'm a little curious now myself."

"You get me that information, and I'll tell you all about it."

Chad caught her up on the gossip going around the station. Some of the names were new. Sarah would only get more out of touch the longer she stayed away from Pittsburgh.

When she hung up, she turned her attention back to the computer. After some digging, she found the people behind U-Stor. The names didn't mean anything to her: one was a local businessman, one was dead—according to the obituary she found online—and one had retired to Florida, like former sheriff Harding. She could do more research, but she wanted to ask Lanford if any of these people meant something to him.

She checked online to find out what had happened to the cousin. He'd died, leaving a good-sized estate, so he shouldn't have needed the Davies property here in Pennsylvania. His death was not unexpected at his age, and she noted the names of those who survived him. The possibilities that they'd have any pertinent information were slim, but…

If nothing panned out, she could let this line of investigation go for now.

Well, unless she got bored.

She nudged Festus with her foot.

"Come on, Superdog. It's lunchtime."

His head lifted, and his tail wagged up and down.

Another busy day.

Lanford walked back to the parsonage, enjoying the sun on his face and the freedom to walk as he pleased. He was free.

He had made the decision not to dwell on the past eighteen years. Bitterness had lived in him long enough, and he refused to give it more space in his life. He had this day, a place to live and work, freedom and, apparently, an unlikely ally.

After he'd cleared his name, he'd be able to make plans for the rest of his future. If he could find who'd really set the fire, it would change what his options were going forward.

He made a sandwich from the food that had been left in the apartment for him, offering a prayer of gratitude. He was sure this would all become normal, forgettable with time, but for now, every moment like this was a gift.

After cleaning up, he headed to the church to talk to the pastor. Harold. Another person God had provided in his new life.

The church was open, so he entered, looking around. The only time he could remember being in this building was for his mother's funeral, and he didn't remember much of that. On the wall was a sign pointing to the basement with Pastor's Office written on it, so he took the stairs down.

Only one door was open. Lanford stood in the doorway and knocked.

Pastor Harold glanced up from his computer, and a smile broke over his face.

"Lanford, come in, come in. Have a seat."

"Thank you." He sat in the shabby chair across the desk from the pastor.

"Do you have everything you need?"

Lanford blinked at the concern in the man's voice. Over the past eighteen years he'd learned to hide his feelings, and to present a stoic front at all times. He'd been cut off from almost all care and affection.

It was hard to accept without becoming emotional, so he called on the habits he'd learned to stay strong. To show no weakness.

"Everything is great. Thank you very much."

The man across from him beamed, as if this was the best news he'd heard all day.

"Excellent. Excellent. We finished those apartments recently, so you're the first to stay there. Please tell me if there's anything we should do to make them nicer. It will help those who come after you as well as yourself."

Lanford had no intention of being ungrateful, but he nodded. If he found something that needed doing, he could do it himself, if he found some tools.

"Is there anything we can do for you?" Harold obviously wanted to help, but he'd already done so much.

Oh, there was one thing.

"Could I make a telephone call?"

"Oh, yes, yes. Certainly. You don't have a phone,

right? I can help you with that, I'm sure. There are a couple of places in town, but maybe you don't want a cell phone? We didn't even think of putting in a land-line up in those apartments—"

"Pastor Harold." Lanford broke in before the man arranged for landlines and cell phones and who knew what else.

The man stopped.

"I will get a cell phone. For the moment, there's only one call I want to make, but there's no rush."

He wanted to call the company his father worked for and ask if he could come and talk to the owner. He'd have to figure out how to get there, since the office was on the outskirts of Pittsburgh. There was no reason to be in a panic until he solved that question.

Harold pushed the phone on his desk toward him. "The phone is here for you, anytime. Well, anytime the office is open. We have to lock up at night—there were some petty thefts, and some of the members were quite upset."

Pastor Harold pushed his chair back.

"Would you like me to step out now, so you can talk?"

Lanford shook his head. "No, it's not a rush. I appreciate the offer. Just let me know when it's convenient."

Harold appeared to restrain himself from leaping out of his chair immediately.

"Okay then. Now, do you want to talk about work?"

"That's why I'm here."

"We lost our custodian recently, and we've been scrambling to fill in, but we didn't grasp what all he did. It wasn't just cleaning the building, but the yard work and the repairs... Is that something you could do?"

As an ex-con, there was very little Lanford would refuse to do. Certainly not honest work.

"I can do that. Tell me what has to be done and where the tools are to do it."

Again, that beaming smile from Pastor Harold.

Lanford would think it was fake, that no one could be that good. But he'd found the same spirit in the prison, and he knew it could be real. He was sure it was for Harold, like it had been for Anton.

He followed Pastor Harold as he led Lanford to where he could find the cleaning supplies and tools.

God had provided this for him, which made him believe that clearing his name and finding out the truth about the fire was the right thing. He prayed that he could manage his mission without opening the door to bitterness or revenge.

It was going to take a lot of prayer.

Chapter Five

Sarah spent the rest of her day dealing with calls that came in. An elderly driver had hit the gas pedal instead of the brakes and run into a wall. She played referee for a dispute where two neighbors in a long-standing property disagreement were complaining about lawn decorations.

A typical day.

She returned to the station and reviewed the file for the Davies arson case again, checking for any relevant information she'd missed, any questions unanswered.

If someone had framed Lanford, they'd probably driven to his place to set the fire, but by the time the fire department, police and ambulance had all been there, it was impossible to check for tire tracks. The house had been completely destroyed. Investigators found an accelerant had been used—which fit with the gas can found near Lanford.

The can, it was later revealed, came from the Davieses' garage. All of the family's fingerprints had been identified on the can. Someone could have pressed Lanford's hands to the canister, or he could have carried it that day or even weeks before.

The lighter in Lanford's pocket was generic, a drugstore item. The sheriff had grabbed it from his pocket without gloves on, so fingerprint evidence was subsequently unusable.

Sarah rolled her eyes when she read that.

If someone had framed Lanford, Roy Harding didn't appear to be on the ball enough to have taken proper steps to prove the case. Based on the skill set Festus demonstrated, Sarah didn't think he was on the ball enough to be part of setting up Lanford, either.

She wondered if she should try to call him again. He hadn't responded to calls or emails about Festus, and she didn't know how he'd react to the news that she was reopening one of his cases, even if it was unofficially. If Lanford had been set up, maybe Harding had been involved.

At the end of the day, there was still the problem of who else would want to do such a thing. Motive wasn't very strong against Lanford, but there was less reason for anyone else.

Sarah was startled to discover that it was past five on a Friday. She was "officially" done for the week but would be on call if something happened. She locked the Davies file in a cabinet, closed up the office and got out the door with Festus after tripping over him only once.

She drove to her home, a small bungalow she'd rented for the year. Her contract with the town was for twelve months, and when she'd signed it, she hadn't been sure she'd stay longer.

She still wasn't sure.

She waved at her neighbor, who was busy in his garden.

Sarah had a condo in the city and had sublet it for the same year. She'd had a small balcony, but she'd never had to deal with lawns and gardens.

Moving here in the winter meant that she hadn't had to deal with maintenance beyond shoveling and throwing down salt. Now, with summer approaching, there was not only grass to mow, but flower beds and a garden to look after.

Arthur, her neighbor, was a retired teacher. He was also a gossip. Last weekend he'd shown her how to dig up the garden bed while telling her stories about the other people who lived on this street. He'd promised to help her prepare the soil this weekend and advise her on what seeds to get for her vegetable garden. She hadn't had the heart to confess that she had a black thumb. She was pretty sure he'd be adopting her garden, as well, so it might not matter.

Arthur was doing something to the rich foliage already apparent around his home. Pruning, maybe? She thought he had scissors or something similar in his hand. She waved and herded Festus into the backyard to do his business. Then she went in the house and pulled out a frozen pizza for dinner.

Tomorrow she'd work on her garden and lead Arthur into discussions about the Davies family. Lanford might not believe his brother or father could have enemies, and he might not want to tell her who he'd upset in the past, but she was a police officer. She could find out her own information.

* * *

Arthur shook his bald head.

"You put in pumpkins and they'll take over the whole patch. That's not good value. You can buy pumpkins from farmers around here if you really want some. Nice beans, on the other hand… They're good value. They give you a lot of food for a small space."

Sarah wasn't fond of beans, but it wasn't worth arguing. She could give Arthur the beans if he liked them that much. Assuming they survived.

She loved pumpkin pie but had never tried to make it from actual pumpkins. That might be more of a challenge than she wanted to attempt. In any case, it wasn't a hill she was going to die on. Beans it was.

"Can I ask you something, Arthur?"

Arthur looked up from where he was kneeling beside her vegetable patch. No, this was going to be Arthur's second vegetable patch. Sarah had no delusions about that.

"You want corn now, right?"

Corn was an improvement over beans, as far as Sarah was concerned, but she shook her head.

"I wanted to know about some people who used to live here in town. I hoped you might remember them."

Arthur pushed himself to his feet. Sarah was tempted to offer assistance, but he'd been upset when she'd done that previously, so she waited for him to straighten.

"I've lived here all my life. I probably knew them."

"The Davies?"

Arthur's eyes widened. "Oh. The Davies. I'd heard Lanford got out of prison and was staying at the parsonage. Is that why you're asking?"

Sarah nodded. She didn't offer further details, but she didn't need to. Arthur was off and running.

"His mother, Marta Davies, was the sweetest girl. She was a few years behind me in school. And Lewis absolutely adored her.

"They were high school sweethearts. Really cute couple. He was more of an athlete, while she was an excellent student. She got a scholarship to go to college.

"Then she got pregnant, so they married and she took some classes at the community college instead. Went to work for a dentist. Riordan was their eldest. He took after his dad, as far as athletics went. He was a runner, and a good one. He got a full scholarship to Penn State for running."

Sarah nodded again, but didn't interrupt to tell him that she knew that part.

"Riordan, or Dan as everyone called him, was a nice kid, super nice, but shy."

"Everyone liked him? No one was jealous or anything?"

Arthur snorted. "Well, of course, some guys resented that he was better at track than they were. But it wasn't anything serious. He didn't brag about his talents, didn't cause trouble—just a good, quiet kid. Not like some."

Arthur sniffed.

"Like some?" It didn't take much to keep Arthur going.

"For example, Billy Robertson."

For some reason that name rang a bell.

Arthur's face showed his opinion of Billy. "That boy had enemies—well, as much as one does in high school. His family were the wealthy ones here in town. Billy was the kid who had the gaming systems everyone wanted and got a car for his sixteenth birthday. And he was the kind to brag. He wasn't a big guy, not very good-looking, so he tried to make up for it by showing off, you know? To make himself more special.

"No one liked him, except Dan. Still not sure why, but Dan was just that nice of a kid. Billy would have had a much rougher go of it at school if he hadn't had Dan as a friend."

Arthur paused, dwelling on the mystery of that long-ago friendship.

"What happened to Billy?"

"Eh, Billy? The whole family moved away—not long after the fire at the Davies place. His parents died in a car accident. He's in the city, probably bragging about his money to everyone now."

She needed to work out why the name Billy Robertson stuck out to her, but she could do that later.

"What about Lanford?"

Lanford opened his notebook and flipped to a blank page.

Dear Anton:

He tapped his pen on the table, and finally continued.

I hope things are going well for you. I can tell you've been praying for me, because things are going well here.

The pastor the chaplain referred me to has provided a place to stay and given me work at the church. The place isn't fancy, but they stocked it up with food and towels and sheets and things, so I'm good to go.

The work is mostly cleaning and taking care of the church and parsonage. It's all stuff I can handle, and doesn't cause any stress, so I'm happy with that.

I worry about the pastor. He's almost too good to be true. He keeps asking if he can do more for me. I know some guys that would take advantage of him, so tell the chaplain to be careful who he sends this way. I'd hate to see the guy ripped off.

Lanford did worry about Pastor Harold. He'd let Lanford use his office for a phone call, and Lanford could have been calling anyone. Harold had offered him keys for the buildings, in case Lanford needed access if there was an emergency.

Lanford had declined. If something went missing, he didn't want to be one of the people with access to the building outside of business hours.

Lanford wasn't inspired to find ways to take advantage of the pastor or the church. He wanted to sit Harold down and explain to him what the real world was like. But he also knew that his own perspective on the real world was formed from eighteen years in prison, and some TV shows and movies.

Still, he was sure his own cynicism was more realistic than Harold's idealism. If nothing else, it put Lanford at more risk. With this much accessibility, if something happened at the church, Lanford could be blamed, and he was an easy scapegoat.

He sighed. Guess it wasn't really stress free, but he wouldn't worry Anton.

Like we talked about, I went to the sheriff's office to explain what I planned to do. It's a new sheriff, which isn't surprising, but it's a woman, which was.

He hadn't paid much attention to her, that first visit. He'd expected the sheriff who'd arrested him would be in the office. He'd been relieved to find someone new, hoping she'd be less biased. He'd also hoped not to have to deal with the sheriff much during his mission, but he'd known that wasn't likely.

He hadn't been surprised she wanted to talk to him again, but he'd been taken aback that she was willing to entertain the idea that he was innocent. Because of that, he hadn't wanted to confess all the stuff he'd done as a kid.

Which was probably stupid. It's not like she couldn't find out. Juvenile records were supposed to be sealed, but he didn't believe that would hold. Once she accessed that information, it would make him more suspicious, less believable.

But when she'd found him standing outside the gates at what had been his old home, he'd noticed her. Noticed that she was pretty, with shiny brown hair in a ponytail, warm brown eyes and freckles over her nose, as if she'd been in the sun.

He liked her voice, and that she was smart. And that made him want to impress her.

That was incredibly stupid. She was attractive, intelligent and obviously capable. He had no idea why she was working here, in a small backwater town, but he was an ex-con. She was a cop. Even if he could prove he was innocent, he was still a guy who'd been in prison for eighteen years.

They were naturally in opposition. And even though he'd noticed she didn't wear a wedding ring, he had nothing to offer her. Nothing but looks that girls used to appreciate.

He gave himself a bit of slack: he had been in prison for eighteen years, and this was the first pretty woman he'd spent time with. He just had to remember that she was helping him and that was as far as it could go. Even that was close to a miracle. He would be stupid to mess it up.

> Also, she's helping me.
>
> At least, that's what she says. I'm suspicious, but she said it would be better for her to know what I'm doing in case some kind of trouble pops up. The kid I was before would be nothing but trouble, but I hope this time I can behave. The only trouble I want is for the person who set that fire. And like we talked about, not for revenge, but so that he pays for what he did, legally.
>
> I called the company my dad worked for. Dad's boss, Mr. Dawson, is retired, but I can go talk to him, when I can get a ride to Pittsburgh. Not sure when that will be.

It had been a shock to find out Marvin Dawson had retired. In his head, he still expected that the world was the same as the one he'd left eighteen years ago. But everything had changed.

Yet another reminder of what he'd lost.

Yes, he'd lost eighteen years, but he'd been on a bad

path. And when he'd gone to prison, he'd found the best cellmate he could have asked for. Thanks to Anton, he'd been protected from some of the worst that happened in a prison. Anton was big and scary. He spent a lot of his time working out, and it showed.

Not that Anton got in fights or tried to bully others. Anton was a Christian.

It had taken a few years for Lanford to take that step himself, but it had changed his life, for the better. If he'd stayed on the path he'd been on in his teens, he could be in much worse trouble. Probably would be.

He was free now. He vowed not to waste that gift.

> I hope you get to read this. I pray for you, and the guys in our Bible study group.
> Lanford

Lanford carefully tore the page out of the notebook. He'd need to buy some stamps and envelopes. Harold had some in his office, but Lanford wasn't going to ask for more from Harold.

He flipped back to the beginning of the notebook. The part where he'd listed the consequences of the fire that night.

He updated his notes with what he and Sarah had done. He didn't list anything under number four, the people who'd want him in prison. He hadn't started on that alternative yet. He'd also yet to apologize to the people he'd hurt. He realized, again with a shock, that some of them might not even be alive, and some he suspected were gone from this town.

The last item? He had no idea how to deal with that. If someone wanted to kill him, he didn't have a clue who it could be. If they still wanted him dead, he didn't have much to prevent them. Except God.

"I will both lay me down in peace, and sleep: for thou, Lord, only makest me dwell in safety."

With that, Lanford changed for bed, and lay down and slept.

Chapter Six

Sarah rotated her attendance at Sunday morning services among all the churches in town. She would have preferred to attend one church, but she didn't want to show favoritism that would lead anyone to believe she was biased for or against anyone in her jurisdiction. She varied her attendance, so that it didn't look as deliberate as it was.

Some Sundays she didn't feel God's presence as much as others, but if nothing else, the chance to sit and make space for God was a good thing.

This week she purposely went to her favorite of the local churches. It so happened to be the one where Lanford was currently working and residing. Her instinct might tell her that he was exactly who he presented himself as, but her instinct was not infallible.

She remembered her neighbor's description of Lanford.

"He was a good-looking boy. I figure the best-looking kid in town at that time. All the girls admired him, for sure.

"It wasn't just the students, either. He got away with

a whole lot. When I was teaching, I saw him around the high school when he was still too young for the place. He was trouble. Not serious trouble, mostly pranks and jokes, and people would forgive him just about anything. He'd smile, flash his dimples, and people were ready to let him get away with whatever.

"Then his mother died. That was just before he started high school, so I saw how it affected him. His dad, well, he'd always been a trucker, away for days, but they'd been a happy family. His dad just closed up after Marta died, though.

"I think those boys lost both parents, in many ways, after she passed. Lewis kept working, so he was away for days at a time. Then a couple of years later, Dan went off to Penn State, and Lanford was left on his own.

"Legally, I know, he was old enough, but that's when he started to get into real trouble. Vandalism—he was responsible for a lot of graffiti at the school. We heard of kids drinking, even some drugs, and I'm sure Lanford was part of that.

"Didn't stop the girls, though, and he could still get away with things. But it was different. I remember, freshman year, he was late on an assignment. He told me he'd left it in his dad's truck, so he couldn't get it for a few days.

"Then he gave me that cheeky smile. Problem was, I'd heard him talking with some of the other kids, and I knew he was lying. He didn't get away with it, not that time, and not with me, but he did get away with a lot.

"By senior year, he wasn't even trying. He lied to my face, told me he'd get the assignment in tomorrow and then smiled. But it was a smirk with no humor behind it. He just didn't care. By then he knew what he could get away with. Didn't work with many of the teachers by then, but there was no one to rein him in.

"I always felt sorry for him. Well, until the arson. I don't believe he meant to kill his family, but he was on a path to trouble, and his family paid the price."

Sarah had no reason to doubt what Arthur had said. She had no knowledge of the boy Lanford had been. The man she'd talked to had been very different, but it had been many years since he was the high school troublemaker, and he'd been through a lot.

She sent up a quick prayer of apology. She was sitting in church, and her attention wasn't on the sermon. Which was a shame because she appreciated Harold's sermons.

Instead, she was watching Lanford a couple of rows ahead.

She wasn't the only one.

He'd been a very good-looking boy, there was no doubt. There were pictures of him in the file in her office from the night of the fire. He'd been shocked, hungover and still noticeably attractive.

He was also a good-looking man, but the pull was different.

She had no idea about whether he still had the dimples because he didn't smile. He had the silent, broody thing going in full force. And she wondered what that might do, here in this small town where he had a history.

She'd come to this service, in simple truth, to check if he was going to do as he'd claimed the first day she'd met him in her station. He'd said he was sober and going to church.

She had reached out to get information on the cousin in Australia, as she'd told Lanford, but she'd also tapped some contacts she had in the judicial system to find out what he'd been like as a prisoner. She was waiting to get those reports back. She also knew that prison was a different world, and people would and did behave differently there.

Checking on whether Lanford was in church was a quick way to verify how he might behave on the outside. No ex-con was going to tell a cop that he was planning to break the law, but what one said and what one did could contradict.

Lanford was exactly where he said he'd be. In a pew, at church. She could ask Harold about him, but Harold would put the best possible spin on the situation.

She wasn't clergy, she wasn't social services—she was the law. That had been beaten into her brain recently. She needed a clear head and an objective mind.

She would do nothing to make his path more difficult, but her job was to protect all the citizens of this town, not just one.

Yet her gaze kept wandering toward him.

His attention was focused on Harold, and he followed all the elements of the service closely. From her vantage point, she could see the other congregants, and how they were responding to his presence.

Some anger and suspicion. Some speculation. A few ignored him, probably newcomers or younger people who didn't know his past.

Sarah could try to convince herself that she was, in a sense, working when she watched Lanford and tried to evaluate his sincerity, but she didn't want to lie to herself.

She pictured the attractive prankster who'd used his charm on people, and then the sulky teenager from his file pictures. She couldn't help comparing those to the man in the pew. He was dressed appropriately, behaved impeccably and showed not a smidgen of charm or humor. How tough had prison been on him? Had it changed his total character, or just layered a hard shell over the person he'd been?

None of these thoughts were work related. She wanted to understand him as a person and find out more.

And that was a problem. Because she was supposed to be objective, and she feared she wasn't just losing her objectivity, but that she might not be able to get it back.

Was the sheriff checking on him?

Probably. It would make sense. He was an ex-con, he'd told her he was planning to look into his case, and if she asked about him, everyone in this town would say he'd been trouble.

He didn't even know if she came to church or was just here to see if he had lied.

It shouldn't bother him, but he was relieved, after the service, when she greeted Harold as a friend. She'd been right behind him when he shook hands with Harold, so he was close enough to hear their conversation. It was apparent that she came to church often. But not just here. Harold mentioned being surprised it was "their turn."

Maybe she *was* checking on him.

Maybe she just wanted to talk to him. He didn't have a phone, after all. After talking to Harold, she'd come over to greet him and asked if he'd stop by the station when he had a chance, because she had information for him.

Had her contact found information on Dan?

One of those stabs of grief shot through him. In prison, he'd had to shut that all down. But here, among the places where he'd spent time with his family, that pain was resurfacing.

The town had changed, but not enough to prevent the memories.

He was determined to find justice for his family. To prove that his parents hadn't raised a criminal. To make sure the real killer wasn't free to do more damage.

He'd take all the help this sheriff could provide. He just needed to remember her ultimate duty was to the law. Not to him.

Harold took Mondays off, so Lanford did, as well. He went to meet the sheriff first thing Monday morning.

It was another beautiful day, and he was grateful that he was outside and free to enjoy it. The walk to the office was short. The door was open, so he went in.

There was a whimper, and a brown streak shot to the back room.

The sheriff sighed.

"Thanks for the support, Festus!" she called out, before turning to greet Lanford.

"Mr. Davies." She held out her hand.

He appreciated the respect that demonstrated. She wasn't mocking him.

"You can call me Lanford, or Lan." He repeated the offer, hoping she'd take him up on it. He'd never been called Mr. Davies until he'd been arrested. He'd rather she used his name.

"Okay, Lanford. You can call me Sarah."

Sarah. He liked that name. It suited her.

The dog, however? Its head was now poking around the doorway, eyeing him fearfully.

"Why did you name him Festus?"

Sarah waved Lanford to the seat in front of her desk and sat back down in her own.

"Festus came with the job. The name was already attached to him."

He took a moment to watch the dog. That kept him from noticing how good she looked. He even liked the faint scent that lingered near her. That thought led to trouble, though. It was better to focus on Festus.

"What kind of police work does he do?"

"You just saw it."

His glance shot back to her, waiting to catch the smile and share the joke.

She just shrugged.

"Seriously?"

"Seriously. He came with the job. I've found no paperwork related to him, no training information, and he has yet to answer even one command."

"Then why is he here?"

Sarah sighed. "What else am I going to do with him? The previous sheriff left for Florida before I got the key to this place. He hasn't answered my calls since. I've had to figure out most of this job on my own. Maybe there's some skill Festus has—I tried drug-sniffing, but he wouldn't come near the stuff. He could be a bomb-sniffing dog, or a cadaver dog, but there's not much call for that around here."

Lanford agreed.

"And if you knew he couldn't do any of that stuff?"

Sarah held up her hands and smiled. "He's mine now, for better or worse. And he does have one skill. He's great at tripping. I've only fallen on my behind once, but there have been too many close calls to mention. For the moment, he's my agility training dog. I'm learning to be very agile on my feet."

Festus was staring at them as if he understood, and his tail moved up and down a couple of times.

"Is he wagging his tail?"

Sarah nodded. "He's very talented. But enough about Festus the wonder dog. Let's talk about your project."

Lanford was happy to let the discussion of the dog go.

"You found out something about Dan?" He was curious, but apprehensive. He loved his brother, and he couldn't imagine Dan getting into the kind of trouble that would get himself killed.

Sarah shook her head. "Not yet. I called my guy, and he's working on it. I'll give you a heads-up when I hear from him, but it probably will take some time. I couldn't ask him to deprioritize active cases he's working on. He's doing this as a favor for me."

"I appreciate it." Lanford didn't want to come across as pushy. Sarah was doing *him* a favor, and a bigger one than he could have ever expected.

It wasn't likely that they'd find an answer very quickly. Nothing had popped up eighteen years ago, so this wasn't a surface issue, something easy to find. For the first time he wondered if she would get in trouble for helping him. She said she wanted to find the truth, but that truth could lead to a wrongful conviction and blot on the police department's record.

He should reassure her that he was doing his part, as well, not just waiting for her to do everything.

"I called the company my dad worked for."

Sarah tilted her head. “How did that go?”

“The man my dad worked for, Marvin Dawson, is retired—his daughter is running the business now. But she gave me his phone number, so when I have a chance to head into the city, I’ll ask him to talk to me.”

“I go into Pittsburgh occasionally—maybe you can hitch a ride next trip.”

“Thank you.” He did nothing but accept help from this woman. She was either truly nice, or she was keeping a close watch over him. Or both. He should be careful about how much he accepted from her. If she was to decide to shut down the case, he would have nothing to fight back with.

Nothing concrete, at least.

Sarah gave a quick nod and then pulled out a sheet of paper.

“This is what I’ve come up with so far. This is the list of people who own U-Stor.”

He looked up from the sheet of paper to find her gaze on him. Something moved in his chest. She didn’t have to do this, and she didn’t have to share with him.

Maybe he could trust her. The idea warmed and scared him. The list of people he trusted was short.

She passed the paper to his side of the desk.

“Any of those names sound familiar?”

Chapter Seven

Sarah watched Lanford as he reached for the list of names.

After just a few days here in Balsam Grove, his complexion was gaining color. He was still guarded but looked less wary.

Sarah was on the opposite side of the judicial system from where he'd been for the last eighteen or more years. That was one thing that bothered her about being a police officer. She didn't want to be against people. If Lanford hadn't burned down his family home, if someone else had and he'd served the time for it, then the justice system had let him down.

She wanted to show that it could work. That it was a system meant to protect, not to harm. That she was like her father.

She pulled her thoughts in. Right now, there was no proof that the system had failed Lanford. If he was guilty, it had only punished him for something he'd done, something that had taken lives. Her instinct might say he was as innocent as he claimed, but she was supposed to be objective.

She couldn't fail on that again, so she'd repeat the message to herself until it stuck.

Lanford was reading the names on her paper.

He frowned.

"I don't know any Thurstons. Are they from around here?"

Sarah had held back the addresses she found. That was objectivity—in case Lanford recognized a name and it led him to consider revenge. She wouldn't make it easy for him to find them.

She shook her head. The Thurstons were from Pittsburgh, business associates of the other owners.

Lanford moved on to the next name.

"The Barstows are local. I never knew them, though. They didn't have any kids my age, and I think he worked at the bank, or something? He used to ride in a car in parades and show up at the Fourth of July."

Wendall Barstow had retired as bank manager five years ago. They spent winters in Florida and hadn't returned to Balsam Grove yet.

"Walter Robertson—he was Billy's father, right?"

Sarah frowned. She hadn't looked far enough into the people to find all their family associations.

"You knew him?"

Lanford's brows were drawn. "If he was Billy's father, then Dan knew him. Dan and Billy were friends."

The pieces clicked in her head. Her neighbor Arthur had told her about Riordan befriending the bullied rich kid. That was why the name Robertson had been familiar.

"Were there other Robertsons in town?"

Lanford shook his head slowly. "Not when I was here. The Robertsons had a lot of money, I remember, and people thought that's why Dan was friends with Billy. It wasn't, though. Billy was picked on a lot, and Dan wanted to stand by him.

"I never liked Billy, but he and Dan were pretty tight."

Well, no motive there.

"Can you think of any reason the Robertsons would have invested in a storage facility that could relate to you?"

Lanford lifted his head and shrugged. "Not really. Billy liked Dan, and I'm sure his folks did, as well. Everyone liked Dan."

She heard the sadness in his voice. His lips were pressed tightly together, as if he was holding something back. Or holding something in.

By all accounts, Dan had been an excellent young man. Lanford, with no family remaining, must miss him. And if Lanford hadn't lit that fire, then someone else had.

So far, they hadn't found any reason. They were looking into the pasts of the father and son, but nothing indicated they had crossed anyone. There was a very good chance that Lanford, the boy who'd been getting into trouble, might be the indirect cause, if not the direct one.

"I'm sorry for your loss, Lanford. Your brother and father were good people."

He glanced away and swallowed. "Thank you. They were."

Sarah reminded herself that she had no reason to trust Lanford. But looking at him, there was no doubt that Lanford grieved his family. If he had set the fire, she was sure he'd had no idea his family was in the house.

She leaned back in her chair, reaching for some distance, some physical distance even though her mental distance was the problem. She tried to put her cop face on.

Lanford was still examining the list.

"Did you talk to any of these people to ask why they built U-Stor?"

Sarah shook her head.

"The Thurstons are a wealthy family in Pittsburgh. Influential people don't like to be bothered without good reason. The Barstows haven't returned from Florida yet, so I was waiting to see if you thought they were a potential link."

"That makes sense, but Billy's parents should be here. They knew Dan, so they might want to help."

"They're dead, Lanford."

His eyes widened. If the news didn't surprise him, he was a good actor.

"All of them? Is Billy dead, too?"

"Walter Robertson died in a car crash a couple of years after U-Stor was built. Billy is alive, but he married and moved to Pittsburgh.

"Would Billy know anything about his father's business?"

Lanford shrugged.

"Billy was Dan's friend, not mine. They never hung out at our place. Billy's place was nicer, and Billy was a snob."

Sarah knew she'd reacted, because Lanford's gaze moved to her again.

It was the first unkind thing she'd heard him say about a particular person.

"Ask around. No one could stand Billy except Dan. Even Dan was sorrier for him than anything else, so they weren't together all the time."

"Billy was a loner?"

Sarah was grasping at straws. Why would Billy set fire to his only friend's house?

But Lanford was shaking his head again.

"No, people hung out with Billy because he had money." Catching the expression on her face, he continued. "Billy got a brand-new sports car when he turned sixteen. His family had the biggest swimming pool of the few we had here. Billy would throw parties, and people sucked up to him to get invites, back before he went to college.

"Before that, before Billy learned how to use his money to his advantage, he used to get beat up for showing off his stuff. Dan stood up for him, but he told Billy to tone down the bragging so that people wouldn't hate him.

"Billy had lots of people around him, but they were using him, all except Dan. Dan couldn't go to the parties because he was in training or helping Dad on some of the long delivery runs. Dan was the guy who'd check up on Billy when the parties were over."

The door to the sheriff's station had opened while Lanford was speaking.

A man walked through the door. He wasn't tall, but he had more than enough confidence to make up for that. His clothes were expensive, his hair styled with every strand in place, and the cologne that came with him smelled of money.

The man didn't waste a glance on Sarah. He was staring at Lanford, and his expression broadcast his hatred.

"You're right. Dan was the one decent person in this crap town."

The man's nose wrinkled, as if he smelled something he didn't like.

"I heard you were back, Lan. I couldn't believe you'd dare show your face here after killing Dan."

Billy had changed.

That was a stupid thought. In eighteen years, everyone had changed. But Billy had changed more than anyone else he'd seen.

Life had been good to him. It was there in his clothes, in his swagger, in the way he walked in here like he called the shots.

He and Lanford had never been friends, but Billy had never looked at Lanford with hatred. Not like he was now.

Lanford stood, reacting to the threat Billy was projecting.

Billy had been taking care of himself—he seemed fit. But Lanford was still taller, and he'd had a lot of hours to kill and frustration to vent while he was in prison. He'd spent that time working out. Lanford could handle Billy in a fight.

Billy had never been in a prison fight. Those had no rules, except winning.

Lanford unclenched his fists. He wasn't going to get in a fight. Especially not in front of the sheriff.

"Billy." Lanford didn't rebut Billy's accusation. He'd been tried and convicted for that crime. The only way people would believe him innocent was if he could prove it.

"I'm Bill now. What are you doing in here? Arrested again already?"

It seemed Billy had also gained a meanness that Lanford didn't remember from before.

"I'm Sarah Winfrey, the sheriff. You are?"

Sarah had stood and moved toward the newcomer. She'd pulled herself to her full height, which was level with Billy. Bill. Her voice was cold.

Billy turned his attention to her. "I'm Bill Robertson. If you have any problems with this man, I'd be happy to help you out."

"That's generous of you, Mr. Robertson, but I'm more than capable of handling my job on my own."

"I'd heard from people that he—" Bill jerked his chin toward Lanford "—was back and came to warn you about him."

"You must have been very concerned to come all the way to Balsam Grove. You're not local anymore, are you?"

Bill's mouth twitched. "I live in Pittsburgh now, but I have interests all over. I was heading this way when I heard Lanford had shown up again. We have a business locally."

"Would that be U-Stor? I wasn't aware you had any other interests in this community now."

Billy was still posturing, attempting to intimidate Sarah. She didn't flinch.

"Yes, my dad helped build that place. Has there been trouble there? Did that criminal do something to the place? I'll press charges."

"I'm not aware of any problems at the U-Stor facility, but you might have heard before I did. Is there any problem that you came to look into?"

Billy let out a frustrated breath. "No."

Sarah cocked her head. "You're clearly a very successful businessman. I'm a little surprised that you came all this way to warn me about Mr. Davies unless you'd been planning to be here anyway for the storage facility. Does the place have some particular meaning for you?"

Billy's eyes narrowed. "No, it doesn't. It was my father's project. I inherited it when he died. I don't deal with the management of it at all. Nothing to do with me. I was on my way to check out some property in New Castle."

His gaze moved back to Lanford.

"Have you been out to check on your old home, Lan? Return to the scene of the crime? Isn't that what criminals do?"

Lanford stood stiffly.

"Did you get your dad to raze the place to get back at me?"

Bill thrust his chin up.

"I couldn't be bothered to have anything to do with you, Lan. You're garbage. Always were, always will be."

Sarah interrupted, her arms crossed.

"Mr. Robertson, if you aren't checking on your business, then your only reason to take this detour is because Mr. Davies is out of prison. That's a lot of bother."

"I came to warn you."

"That was very…considerate of you. But a phone call wouldn't have sufficed?"

Bill narrowed his eyes.

"Shouldn't you be more worried about a convict showing up in your town, Ms. Sheriff?"

"Mr. Davies has served his time and is on parole. If he breaks the terms of his parole, then I will be involved. So far, he's come by to inform me he's here, and I've seen him in church. None of those things have required any action on my part."

Billy's mouth started to open, but Sarah was still talking.

"I'm a fully qualified law officer, with fifteen years of experience in Pittsburgh. I appreciate it when anyone informs me of a potential issue in the community. But I don't appreciate it if that concern is based on whether I can do my job because of perceived deficiencies resulting from my gender.

"I understand you have ill will toward Mr. Davies because of his crime. However, now that he's served his sentence, any attempt to deal out personal justice will put you on the wrong side of the law."

Billy's anger filled the room.

"He's charmed you, just like he charmed the rest, hasn't he? He could get away with anything, but not murder. Not that time. I'm not letting him get away with anything else."

"I don't plan to let anyone 'get away' with anything illegal, Mr. Robertson, whether it be an ex-convict in this town or a wealthy businessman from the city. This town has been peaceful, and my job is to keep it that way.

"Do you have a problem with that?"

Sarah had moved her hands to her waist, just above her weapon.

Billy drew in a long breath, controlling his temper with difficulty. Finally, he relaxed, and smiled.

"I'm very sorry, Sheriff Winfrey. I was upset when

my wife's family told me that Lanford had been released. It brought back a lot of grief and anger from that time. I apologize for inferring you would be anything but capable and impartial in performing your duties.

"As you noted, I don't live here anymore, and this doesn't involve me. I'll just apologize again and get back to where I belong."

He smiled at Sarah, but she remained in the same position, watching him leave.

The door closed behind him. Sarah dropped her defensive pose.

She turned to look at Lanford. "That was unexpected. I think he would qualify as someone for consequence number four—someone who would have been happy to hurt you."

Lanford shook his head. "He wasn't like that, not back then."

She looked at him. "No? So, this…hatred was a result of your brother's death?"

"I guess. I hardly spoke to Billy before. We didn't run in the same circles."

"He had no reason to harm you, not before the fire?"

"He didn't know anything about me that would upset him."

Sarah frowned, but he didn't add anything more.

He had chosen his words carefully.

He *had* done something that would upset Billy if he'd found out. But he hadn't. And there was no reason for it to be an issue anymore. Lanford didn't need to stir up more trouble, not when Billy was this upset already.

Billy missed Dan, and he was laying that anger on Lanford. That was a burden Lanford would have to bear until he found the real arsonist.

He'd done many things that would make people wish to harm him. But none of them would be worth burning down the house, whether the arsonist suspected he and his family were in there or not.

If someone had beat him up, stolen things from him… That he could understand, and could probably give a listing of those who would be throwing the punches.

Arson and murder were a long way from that.

So who had lit the fire?

Chapter Eight

Sarah sat back down at the desk. Lanford hesitated until she nodded at the chair, and then he sat down across from her.

"We were talking about U-Stor before we were interrupted."

He nodded.

"Well, we know where Billy stands on the company now. Would his father have wanted to build that facility for any personal reason?"

Lanford looked up at her, mouth twisted. "Dan liked Billy's family, so I can't imagine they would have any ill will against him."

Sarah considered. "Maybe...they wanted to adopt him and your dad—"

For the first time, she saw Lanford smile. That smile packed a punch, and she felt it.

"Dan had finished his sophomore year in college. They couldn't adopt him at that point."

The smile faded. "Plus, Dan and Billy weren't hanging out as much together once they got to college. They went to different campuses and Billy had made his own friends. Dan mostly hung out with his track teammates. But Billy still seems pretty upset. They must have kept in touch more than I realized."

Sarah frowned. The storage facility and family property seemed to be dead ends. Which was too bad, because she'd disliked Billy Robertson from the moment he'd stormed into her station.

She reminded herself to be objective. She couldn't do her job if she let her personal feelings bias her actions.

After all, even jerks had rights.

She looked at Lanford. "Do you have a bit more time?"

He raised his brows. "Do I have anything else?"

"I meant, are you needed at the church, or can we go over this case a little longer?"

"I'm off today, I think, unless something comes up. But what about you? Don't you have things to do?"

She waved at the phone. "Have you heard this ring? It's not that busy here. I can scan some more case files into the computer, but it's not pressing. We could review the file together—I'll compare what you remember to what's here, and we'll see if anything was missed."

"I told the police everything I could remember."

"Yes, your statement is in here. But maybe you'll recall something when we go over the file, or maybe something was left out. If we find a discrepancy, we'd have a thread to pull on. That might unravel something interesting."

"I appreciate you taking the time for this."

She bit her lip. She *was* making a special effort. And the reasons were muddled.

There was some professional pride. She'd love to find an answer everyone else had missed. After what had happened in the city, she wanted to feel that she was good at what she did, and that she added more value than she took away.

There was also the fact that she was a little bored at this job, while she wasn't ready yet to return to the city. This case was a distraction, something to keep her busy.

There was the feeling she had that Lanford truly was innocent, and she wanted to find who the real murderer was, because that's why she became a cop.

And if she dealt with this, did all she could, she wouldn't need to spend more time with Lanford, which would be good.

Her neighbor Arthur had talked about how Lanford could charm people. It didn't seem like he was exerting any effort at charming her, but somehow, she was warming to him, more than she should.

So, she'd investigate, find out what she could and then send him on his way. Hopefully by then she'd also have figured out what she was going to do with her life. That was her plan.

She opened the locked side drawer on her desk, where she'd put Lanford's file. She hadn't seen anything in the file that made her sit up and take notice, so the only shot she had was if Lanford could spot something.

Lanford stiffened as she set the thick file on her desk. He was frowning at it. She doubted it was the dog ears and fingerprints on the folder that bothered him.

"It was May 28, which means the anniversary is coming up."

Lanford gave a short nod.

She summarized what was inside: "A neighbor, Sadie Jones, called 911 at 2 a.m., saying she smelled smoke and got up to see flames."

Sarah glanced up, but Lanford was staring at the file, expression wooden.

"The fire department arrived, found you unconscious on the front lawn beside an empty jerry can with remains of gasoline in it. The firefighters called the sheriff and the ambulance. They tried to wake you up but were unable to do so. They found a lighter in your pocket. The EMTs worked on you, found you had inhaled smoke, had some first-degree burns and a bump on your skull. There was also a strong smell of alcohol on your person."

Lanford hadn't responded and was still staring at the file.

Sarah continued. "When they were able to wake you up, you had no memory of what had happened, and vomited. They gave you a Breathalyzer, and you were well over the legal limit for driving."

He had been well over the legal limit for just about anything but passing out.

"You were arrested and charged with arson, as it was found to be deliberately set with gasoline, from the jerry can beside you. The next day they found the bodies, and the charges were upgraded to third-degree murder.

"When you were able to make a statement, you said you came home from a party and fell asleep on the couch. You were not aware your father and brother were home since they'd left to make a delivery—Riordan was working with your father on this run. You woke up to find the house engulfed in flames. You made your way out of the house, fell and hit your head and then woke up after the fire department and police had dragged you away."

She stopped her recitation. He still didn't respond.

"Lanford? Is anything I just said wrong?"

He lifted his head and met her gaze. There was pain in his eyes. Revisiting this had to be difficult.

"No. Those are the facts."

She drew in a breath. "Was there any evidence you can think of, any part of your story that was missed? Anything that was shoved under the rug?"

Lanford swallowed. "I understand why they arrested me, and why they found me guilty. There was no one else around, and no one had cause to set that fire. Including me. But they had to find someone, and I'd been set up nicely."

There was the case for the defense. "If someone else set that fire, they did a stellar job of framing you for it."

His nostrils flared when she said *if*. But her job was to investigate the facts, without bias. There could be a reason Lanford Davies needed to be found innocent of this crime now, something she didn't know.

"The weakest part of the case was motive. That was never going to clear you, but the motive they had was that you all had been talking about setting a fire at the party earlier that night."

Lanford shrugged. "That's what everyone said. But I didn't hear them talking about it."

Sarah flipped over some pages to where she'd posted a sticky note.

"You said you hadn't heard them talking about a fire, that it must have been when you went to 'take a leak.' No one could swear that you were around the bonfire during the arson talk, but no one could say you weren't, either."

His lips twisted. "Well, that part isn't exactly true."

Sarah's stomach clenched. The biggest support of

his innocence was his lack of motive. If he hadn't been part of the arson talk around that bonfire, if he had no reason to think of lighting a building on fire with gasoline, then that would support his contention that he had been set up.

Her voice was tense. "What wasn't true about that? You did hear them talking?"

She could believe he hadn't wanted to kill his family. That maybe even he hadn't planned to burn up his own house. But he'd been drunk, really drunk, and if he'd been considering setting a fire…

"I left the bonfire, like I said. But I wasn't alone, and I didn't go to relieve myself."

The words were reluctant, but she had to wonder if this was a lie. Something he'd come up with in prison. Because an alibi would have been his best shot at clearing his name.

And no one had come forward to say they'd left the bonfire with Lanford.

"So why did you leave, and who did you go with?" Unspoken was *why did you never mention this?*

Lanford fidgeted, pulling at a thread on his shirt.

"There was this girl."

Sarah blinked.

That was not what she'd been expecting.

"She had a boyfriend. We weren't supposed to be fooling around together, but we were."

He shook his head. "She said she wanted to talk to me. I figured she wanted to get serious or break up with her boyfriend, so I was more interested in getting her clothes off than talking. She got mad and left. I took a moment and then went back, as well.

"No one saw us leave the group, no one saw us return. No one could say if we were gone when they were talking about burning the Morrison barn. I didn't say anything before now because it would have just messed up her life, and it wouldn't have helped mine.

"Otherwise, everything you said is right. I just thought I'd make that clear, so you knew what was going on."

Sarah put her hands on the file and studied Lanford. After a glance her way, he looked down again.

"You kept quiet to protect her?"

"I'm not a hero. If it would have saved me, I'd have told. It just didn't seem worthwhile to mess up anyone else's life for nothing."

"That was still a nice thing to do."

He lifted his head and shot her a heated glance. His cheeks were flushed.

"The nice thing would have been to stay away from her. I didn't want anything but sex from her. I was a selfish swine, so not dragging her down was the barest minimum of decency I could do."

"You didn't force her, did you?"

His eyes widened. "No! I wouldn't do that. I—I wouldn't do that."

"So, she wanted to have sex with you?"

His gaze dropped again. "Yes."

Sarah considered. "Did she…pursue you, or did you pursue her?"

His mouth opened, then closed. He finally growled. "What does it matter?"

"I think it goes a long way to reveal character, both hers and yours. If she had a boyfriend and still pursued you, then that tells me she's a cheater and a liar. Since she didn't come forward to try to help you, that probably makes her selfish, especially when you were arrested and tried. I don't think, in this small town, anyone was unaware of what was happening to you."

Lanford frowned at her. "I was a cheater, too."

Lanford hadn't wanted to talk about this with Sarah. It had been silly to hope they could investigate his case without digging up all the messes of his past, but he really hadn't wanted her to hear all the things he'd done.

She didn't know all of it. He wasn't revealing everything. But what he had to tell her was bad enough.

Some of the stupid things he'd done weren't that bad. He'd gotten drunk, he'd spray-painted some rude stuff on people's property and he'd stolen things. Nothing big, because it wasn't about getting the actual object—it was just about attention.

His dad had disappeared after their mother died. Not always physically, but he'd blocked out everything but work, so it was just Dan and Lanford.

Then Dan went to college, and the house was too empty. So, he'd go out, away from the emptiness that was there whether his dad was in the place or not. When the guys suggested burning down an old shed, or having a party, or getting drunk, he'd been up for whatever, trying to get his dad to notice.

It hadn't worked. He'd been conflicted, not wanting to upset his dad some of the time, and sometimes wanting to yell at him.

But what he'd done with Allison had been bad.

Allison didn't just have a boyfriend; she had a fiancé. He should have stayed away from her. But she was the hottest girl in town, and older, and someone had finally wanted him. It had been a balm to his ego, and a lot of fun—the sneaking around had enhanced it somehow—but he hadn't known her or cared for her.

He'd used her. Wasn't it obvious how bad that was?

"No, you weren't a cheater, Lanford, unless you were involved with someone else?"

He shook his head. He hadn't dated one girl. It was too much of an ego stroke to know so many girls wanted to spend time with him. He'd enjoyed being sought out.

Especially by Allison.

"Okay." Sarah was looking at her file again.

"You went away from the bonfire with this girl, she left you and you came back. What happened then?"

"I went home."

She was reading the notes, in all their condemning detail.

"You had a dirt bike, right?"

He had. He'd been too drunk to talk to Allison, but he'd thought he was fine to ride his bike home on the highway. He'd been an idiot.

Sarah looked up at him. "You could have been charged with drunk driving."

He nodded. He wasn't sure why they'd let that one slide. Maybe because murder in the third degree was enough.

"You left your bike on the front drive and went in the house. You didn't go to the garage, didn't see the family vehicle there."

He hadn't. He'd had no idea Dad and Dan had come back from their delivery. They'd expected to be away for five days.

"The phone records show your brother called you but you didn't pick up and he left a message."

"I barely made it to the couch before I passed out."

He was pretty sure he'd been lying halfway off of it when he finally came to.

"The message said that your brother was returning to talk to you about some trouble you were in, something that would mess up your whole life. You never told anyone what that was."

He met her gaze. It was steady, nonjudgmental. It made him want to confess everything.

She must be good at her job. But she wasn't good enough to dig up things he didn't know.

"I didn't tell anyone because I have no idea what he was talking about."

Her brows raised. "Not a clue?"

He'd had a lot of time to think about it. To try to figure out what Dan was so upset about, something so bad it had brought him and Dad back from their delivery. Back to their deaths.

"You've probably heard the trouble I was getting into. It wasn't good, and I wasn't going anyplace he'd want me to, but there was nothing new. Nothing that serious."

He'd wondered if Dan was upset about Allison, but they'd kept their relationship secret.

He'd have heard from his friends if word had gotten out about him and Allison. His friends would have praised him. But he and Allison had been very careful because Allison didn't want to upset her fiancé. And it was stupid, but it would cause her more trouble than it would Lanford. It wasn't fair, but there was a double standard. Lanford would be seen as a player, and she'd be called names like slut. She wouldn't have said anything.

"Drugs?"

He clenched his jaw. "Only for fun, I never dealt

anything, and it wasn't any more of a problem than anything else."

"Maybe someone told your brother it was?"

He raised his palms. "Maybe. Maybe someone told him I was going to rob the bank or blow up the school or any stupid thing. I don't know, and no one ever came up with anything."

Sarah's eyes narrowed.

"Then someone is holding back. Maybe the killer told Dan a story to get him to return that night. Maybe their problem was with Dan."

A part of him hoped that was right, that Dan hadn't died for something Lanford did, but it was hard to believe. Dan had been a decent guy. No cover-up, no agenda, just a thoroughly good guy.

"I've considered it." He'd thought about a lot of possibilities. "But unless your friend finds something out at Penn State, there's nothing. People loved Dan."

Sarah huffed. Maybe she was frustrated with him. Maybe she didn't want to deal with this anymore. He wouldn't blame her, but he wasn't stopping.

"Well, we've found two things in your favor. Maybe three."

"That storage place, that it's not doing well."

Sarah nodded. "And your brother had a reason for coming back that night. Someone knows that reason, and they've kept that a secret."

That almost sounded…hopeful.

"And the third thing?"

"You're either lying, or you're kind enough to save a woman from getting into trouble, even when it might have helped your case."

"It wouldn't have."

"Even so, it speaks to some good in your character. Maybe we should talk to her. I could reach out if you don't want to."

Lanford shook his head. "There's no point in blowing up her life. She can't help."

Sarah stared at him, but he kept his gaze down. She sighed.

"Let's see if there's anything else."

Sarah dug through the reports with him for another hour, but they couldn't find anything. Lanford excused himself. He didn't want to take up all her time and get her in trouble. He was selfish and wanted her to keep on helping him.

Also, he didn't want to have to dig into more details about the rotten punk he'd been. Stupid, but she thought he'd shown some signs of decency. Might as well not shatter that belief.

Chapter Nine

Sarah folded up the Davies file and returned it to the drawer in her desk.

Maybe it would turn out to be nothing, but there were enough inconsistencies to make her think Lanford could be right.

It was too bad Billy Robertson hadn't been part of the storage facility plan. He had enough hatred for Lanford to have caused him harm. He must have been very attached to Lanford's brother to still be this upset. Even going so far as to detour all the way to Balsam Grove to check out what Lanford was doing. According to Arthur, he'd had reason to be upset.

Yet, even if Lanford had been the one to set the fire, as was the truth as far as anyone knew, no one believed Lanford had deliberately set out to injure or kill his family. It was a drunken prank gone very wrong, and one that had hurt Lanford more than anyone.

Billy's anger was more than she'd have expected.

Had Billy learned something about Lanford? Had he been the one to warn Dan? If so, why hadn't he come forward to share what it was?

She didn't think he'd tell her if she asked him.

Sarah shook her head. She might never find the answers to these questions. Chad might have found out something about Dan at college.

Maybe she should ask about the Davies family around town. Eighteen years was a long time, though. There might only be a limited number of people remaining who could talk to her about Lanford and his family.

She'd yet to ask her predecessor for his insights, fearing he'd be defensive about his case. But she was running out of leads. She sent off a quick email, hoping Roy would respond to this one, even if he'd refused to answer her previous questions.

She locked her desk drawer, determined to set aside any further questions about the Davieses until she had more information. Her phone rang and she answered, hoping there might be something interesting going on in town to keep her busy.

Apparently, there was. Her caller was complaining about kids causing trouble at Pastor Harold's church.

"Festus, come on. Let's see how you do with crowd control."

Festus crawled out from under her desk, tail tucked tightly between his legs. She clipped on the leash and encouraged him out to the sheriff's SUV.

It took two minutes to arrive at the church.

The kids were there holding up signs. It was a protest.

She stopped the vehicle and opened her door.

"Coming, Festus?"

He wrapped his paws over his head. Sarah rolled

her eyes. Add crowd control to the long list of things Festus didn't do.

She crossed the road to the dozen or so high school students standing on the church lawn, holding up handmade signs.

"Hey, guys, what's going on?"

One girl marched forward, jaw up, eyes sparking.

"We're protesting. You have no right to stop us. We're recording this, and we'll report any signs of police brutality."

Sarah studied her. She suspected the girl would appreciate a bit of oppression, for the excitement value if nothing else. But she could almost taste the good intentions exuding from the small crowd.

She looked around. On the other side of the street, an elderly gentleman sat on his front porch, arms crossed. There was her snitch.

She glanced back at her protesters.

"You guys staying hydrated? It's getting toward summer, and it can be hot."

Wary eyes watched her. "Yeah, we have water."

"Let me see those signs."

"You have no right to confiscate them."

Sarah shook her head. "No, you don't have to give them to me—I just want to read them."

The teens looked at each other, then spread out to show their signs. Some were on cardboard, some on poster paper, one was the back of a For Sale sign.

Sarah read them. Big cities were having similar protests, and these kids just wanted to show their support. In this small town, though, there wasn't a lot they could do.

"I don't see any swearing. I like how you shortened *frustrating*, very clever. Any spelling mistakes?"

"Is there a law against spelling mistakes?"

"Not that I'm aware of, but my grade ten English teacher was a terror. I'm still worried about her finding out that I've made a public mistake.

"But you're all good. If you have any problems, give me a call."

She walked over to the man watching, almost vibrating with his disapproval. He started to yell as soon as she was within speaking distance.

"Aren't you going to stop them? They should be in school. Not this foolishness."

This man was more likely to instigate a problem than her protesters.

"They're on church property, so only Pastor Harold can ask me to move them. I'm not a truant officer, so it's up to their parents and the school if they're skipping classes. What they're doing isn't breaking any laws, so I'm going back to the station.

"If you see anyone hassling them, give me a call. That might be something I need to deal with."

Anger flared in the man's eyes, but she wasn't an elected official, not for this one-year interim position. No one had run when Ron Harding retired, so she wasn't worrying about votes. She had a lot more sympathy for the kids than for this man.

Festus welcomed her return with relief, and she drove slowly to the station. Apparently, the excitement was over for the day, unless her snitch turned his hose on the protesters. That would give them a story, and she might have a chance to use her handcuffs.

The Davies case still tickled her brain, but she resolutely set it aside and decided on more digitizing for the afternoon. Mentally, she urged Chad to get busy with Penn State, but her telekinetic powers were as useless as Festus right now.

Sarah went to the town diner for lunch. The place had good coffee, terrible decor and food that ranged from good to questionable. Sarah had now, after several months, figured out that the simpler the item on the menu, the better. She ordered a BLT with a salad on the side and looked around the diner for prospective gossips.

There weren't many customers now. People tended to eat right at noon, but Sarah had been called out for the protest, then dropped her vehicle and Festus at the station. She'd missed the midday rush.

When her waitress brought out her sandwich, Sarah nodded at the chair across from her.

"Do you have a minute?"

The waitress was an older woman named Phyllis, whom Sara had chatted with at one of the local churches. She yelled back to her husband, the cook.

"Jeff, I'm taking five."

She returned to the counter to pour herself a coffee, then sat down across from Sarah. Sarah noted that the customers still lingering over their own meals were paying attention.

"So, what's up, Sheriff?" Phyllis took a drink of her coffee, then leaned back, stretching out her legs with a sigh.

"You've lived in Balsam Grove for a while, right?"

"All my life." She didn't sound excited about it.

Sarah quirked up a tiny smile. “How do you feel about gossiping?”

Phyllis grinned. “If you’re the one asking, it’s my civic duty, now, isn’t it? Is this about the kids over at the church?”

Sarah shook her head. “No, I’m interested in something from a while back. The Davies family?”

There was a moment of silence in the diner. Every head turned her way. Jeff even came out from the kitchen.

“Is this about Lanford?” the waitress asked.

“Indirectly. I have a lot of information on him in the files. I was wondering about his father and brother.”

Her brows creased. “Why?”

One of the men at another table spoke up. “I heard Lanford still says he’s innocent.”

Jeff snorted. “He was a punk. If he didn’t do it, then who did? Tell me that?”

Sarah broke in. “Lewis and Riordan didn’t have any enemies?”

Everyone looked at Sarah again but it was Phyllis who spoke. “Enemies? No one around here has enemies. I mean, Bella and Nadia would each be happy to see the other one leave town, and when Billy Robertson moved away, we all said good riddance, but that’s as bad as it gets.

“Lewis and Dan were good people. Nobody wished any harm on them. The whole town threw a party for Dan when he left on that scholarship. We were proud of him. And his dad, after his wife died, he never said boo to a goose.”

A voice chipped in from the back table.

“She was a saint, that’s what Marta, his wife, was.”

That all supported the information Sarah had and didn't help her with this case at all.

"Neither of them dated anyone here, had any money troubles...?"

It was a long shot, but it was all Sarah had.

Jeff pointed a finger at her. "Anyone tells you something like that about Lew or Dan, they're lying. They were good men, and it was a tragedy that we lost them. If Lan's back here, trying to stir up trouble, you don't pay any attention to him. No one would have set that fire to hurt either of them."

She decided to take the bull by the horns.

"What about Lanford? Would someone have set the fire to hurt him?"

The locals exchanged glances.

"Lanford was getting in a lot of trouble," said Phyllis.

"I heard he was going to be expelled," Jeff added.

"Nah," said the guy in the back. "He'd charm those teachers every time they caught him. The sheriff, though—he wasn't going to be charmed. Lan was going to get caught, and then—"

The speaker broke off, undoubtedly realizing that Lanford *had* been caught.

The conversation petered out. The town might like to gossip, but she was a newcomer, and they'd only speak so much.

"Just one last question." Sarah finished her meal and pushed the plate aside. "Lewis and Riordan were supposed to be on a delivery for another five days. Does anyone know why they came back that night?"

Phyllis pursed her lips. Her husband scratched his neck. The other diners leaned back.

"Did the school call about Lan?" Someone hazarded

the guess, but the tone revealed it was nothing but a guess.

"Lanford was running all over town on that bike of his. Maybe someone complained about it?"

Jeff shook his head. "They wouldn't come back from a job for that. And the school didn't call—I heard the sheriff asked."

Sarah dropped money on the table to cover her meal and a generous tip. "So no one knows the answer?"

Sarah wasn't an expert at reading faces and body language, but with what skills she had, she doubted anyone was lying as they all denied knowing why the Davieses had returned that night.

She'd keep asking but she suspected the answer was either a mystery to everyone in town or was a long-buried secret held by only one person.

Lanford screwed in the last corner of the switch plate and then flicked the light on. It glowed with a soft, warm light. He allowed himself a smile.

It was a simple fix, but very satisfying.

"Amazing."

Pastor Harold appeared behind him, his honest face beaming.

Lanford stepped aside, and the pastor reached over, turned the switch off and then on again.

"I've been frustrated by that switch for a year now."

"It's not that hard to fix it."

Harold sighed. "Probably not, but it's not a talent I possess."

Lanford wondered why he hadn't asked someone to do it for him, but his years in prison had taught him not to ask questions. Lanford was just grateful that he had work to do, and that he'd been able to so easily impress this man who was helping him out.

"I'm thrilled to have that light working, but I actually came to ask you if you wanted to take a break. I have some scones, and there's coffee on."

Lanford knew Harold was a good, kind man, but he didn't believe this was a random talk. He appreciated the gesture, but he was expecting this was the prelude to something. The way things had gone for him, he didn't expect it would be good.

He followed Harold to his office, where the pastor fussed over Lanford, giving him a scone and some coffee. When he was sure Lanford had everything he could provide him with, he sat in his own chair behind his desk. He met Lanford's eyes.

The man sighed. Lanford braced himself. He was going to be asked to leave.

"I'm glad to share some food with you, and I do need to get to know you better, but I asked you here for a reason."

Lanford nodded.

Harold looked unhappy. He was definitely going to ask Lan to leave.

"I'm a little slow to get the local gossip. I'm not a fan of people talking about others behind their backs. I may have been a little vehement about that, so people are slow to tell me things."

Lanford wondered what Harold had been told. He thought Harold already knew the worst. After all, Lanford's crimes weren't a secret.

"I knew you were getting out of prison, but I wasn't aware that you were investigating your case."

It was a different way to express it. But Lanford would be honest with the man.

"I didn't set the fire, and I want to find out who did."

Harold looked even more unhappy. Some of his congregants must have been complaining. Lanford was sorry, because Harold was a truly Christian man, and he hated to make his life more difficult.

Harold drew in a breath and gazed at Lanford. "Why? And what do you plan to do if you discover the guilty party?"

Lanford took a moment to compose his thoughts. He didn't have much planned past finding out what had really happened that night.

"I would like my name to be cleared." His future would have more options if he wasn't an ex-con, but instead, a wrongly imprisoned innocent man. Only *innocent* wasn't the right term. Innocent of this one thing, at least.

"And the person who did this? Should not be able to do it again." The person had not only destroyed the Davies home and killed his father and brother, they'd let him go to prison for it.

"Do you plan to make sure personally that this other person is unable to do it again?" Harold waved his hand. "Let me make that clearer—are you looking for revenge?"

Lanford leaned back. He should have expected this question, but he hadn't, not from Pastor Harold.

"No, sir."

Harold looked skeptical.

Lanford wanted to be able to stay in the apartment over the parsonage. He wanted to make himself useful around the property. He appreciated this chance to dig into what had happened eighteen years ago, and he believed he was following God's path when he did this. Not only had He provided this place to stay and work to do, but the sheriff was helping him.

That was more than he'd even thought to ask for.

But Harold wanted reassurance that Lanford was not here to do damage. Lanford took a breath, and decided it was time to share.

After all these years, he found it difficult to do. He breathed a quick prayer and prepared to tell Harold what had changed him.

"When I was arrested and tried eighteen years ago, I was shocked. Grieving. I didn't completely understand what was going on.

"Then I wound up in prison. That was another shock, but the grieving turned to anger."

Lanford shifted uncomfortably.

"I got into some fights. I lost most of them, but I didn't care. I just had so much hate and anger inside that I had to get it out.

"It could have been really bad for me. But my cellmate was a lifer. He was a big guy, kept some of the threats away from me, but most importantly, he was a Christian."

He could sense Pastor Harold's interest picking up in his story, but the man stayed quiet at his desk, hands folded on some paperwork.

He was a great listener. A good trait for a pastor.

"For the first couple of years, Anton had a hard time with me. I mocked him when he read the Bible and prayed. It was obvious to me that God, if He existed, didn't care much for me or for Anton."

Lanford could feel his expression softening as he

thought of the big, tough, patient man who'd been his cellmate.

"Anton prayed for me, protected me and took my abuse until I couldn't stand it anymore. He showed more of God's love to me than I'd ever seen in my life."

Lanford smiled. He couldn't help it when he thought of Anton.

"He beat me. Not physically. He just won me over. Next thing I know, I'm reading the Bible and praying with him. And we talked.

"As we got closer to when I was going to be released, we talked about what I was going to do. We prayed about it. We made sure I was going to do this right."

They had talked a lot. Prayed a lot. Lanford had years of stored-up anger and resentment.

"If the fire hadn't happened, I probably would have still ended up in prison, this time for something I *had* done. I was going down a bad road. And despite that, God took what was a terrible experience and worked some good from it.

"I'm not doing this for revenge, because God won't bless that, and because then I could end up in prison again. That's something I don't want."

"'Vengeance is mine,'" Pastor Harold quoted.

"Exactly."

"I'm very relieved to hear that. You do have a lot to be bitter about. You're so quiet, I wasn't sure if you were sitting on a volcano of negative emotions, waiting to blow when you found out who had harmed your family."

Pastor Harold spoke as if it was proven that Lanford was innocent. It touched Lanford, more than he could say.

It made him want to protect the man. He was too

trusting. He hadn't seen the other side of people, the way Lanford had. Prison had changed him. It had brought him faith, but it had also exposed him to some of the worst kind of people, on both sides of the bars.

But Harold trusted God, and Lanford couldn't deny him that. He'd just be handy in case God wanted to use him to protect Harold.

"Are you okay if I stay at the parsonage, keep working for you?"

"Oh, of course. I wasn't going to ask you to leave, no matter what your intentions were. Now I don't have the burden of praying you out of seeking revenge, which is a relief. I'm not good at confrontation."

Harold bit his lip and looked nervous. Lanford, who had relaxed, tensed again.

"Would it be all right if I… I mean, you can say no, but…could I pray with you?"

Lanford could count on one hand the number of people who cared enough to pray for him. Anton was one. The prison chaplain was another.

Now Harold.

For a moment, he wondered about Sarah, the sheriff. She came to church. It might just be a political gesture, but maybe she was a believer. Would she pray for him?

Lanford brought his wayward thoughts under control. He bowed his head, letting Harold speak the words.

It did look like God was blessing this venture.

Chapter Ten

Sarah didn't hear from Chad or Lanford for several days. It shouldn't have been a problem. She blamed the lack of other work for the way her mind continued to wander to the Davies file.

She'd spoken to a few other people around town and found nothing that could be called a lead from any of those conversations. Lewis Davies had been a quiet man. His wife had been well loved, and her passing mourned. Everyone agreed that Lewis had been devastated by that loss and had thrown himself into work.

The community understood, but also blamed him for Lanford's escalating wildness. After Riordan left for school, Lanford started to spiral out of control.

Dan had been as beloved as his mother. His friendship with Billy was constantly mentioned as an indication of how good a young man he'd been.

There was no mention of misdeeds, love affairs or anything negative, except that they'd left Lanford mostly on his own, to Lanford's detriment.

People did tend to remember only good or bad in people who'd died, but if that was the case, the bad in the Davies family was so well hidden she might not be able to dig it up. As well, no one she talked to believed anyone but Lanford was responsible for the fire.

When it came to Lanford's list, the only item that might support his innocence was his own bad behavior. If he hadn't lit that fire, then it seemed whoever did had wished Lanford harm.

Sarah had received a couple more calls about the kids protesting, but there had been no other fallout. Pastor Harold had been pleased with her response, though her job was not to make the pastor happy. It did support her belief that she was doing her job in a way that would please God, however, and that was important to her.

Finally, when she thought she couldn't digitize another file, she got a call from Chad. He'd heard back from his contacts at the school and suggested they meet up and talk the next time she came into the city.

Maybe Sarah should have insisted he give her the information over the phone, but she was short on work and long on curiosity. She set up a day when he was free to meet her and decided she should let Lanford know.

After all, it was always possible that he'd get impatient and try to find out that information on his own. And if she was being honest, she wanted to see him.

She drove over to the church. She noted that the protesters were gone. She parked her vehicle and spotted her quarry working on some plantings around the steps to the church.

The slam of her door brought his head up. He stood, dusting his hands off on his pants.

She was impressed again by his physical presence. He was tall and well muscled, moving with a natural grace. She suspected if his life had been different, he might have been an athlete like his brother.

His complexion was browning from the time he was spending outdoors. The church lawn was smooth and weed free, and the flowers Lanford was planting were in a freshly turned bed, providing a cheery note.

Pastor Harold wouldn't be getting complaints about the work Lanford was doing.

"Sheriff." He greeted her, a questioning expression on his face.

"Lanford. The place looks much better. I assume that's all you, because I know Pastor Harold has a black thumb."

A smile crossed his face, revealing dimples. The wary, reserved man she'd met the first day in her station was warming up. She doubted he'd ever be as open as the kid he'd been, but he was overcoming some of the chains of his past.

She wanted to prove his case, bring him back to the person he should have been, as much as she could. But she had to be careful. Did she have some natural weakness that inclined her to help people on the wrong side of the law? Would she end up bending the rules, like her grandfather?

She was getting too involved.

"I enjoy working outside." He glanced around. "After prison, it feels really good."

"I just heard from my friend, the one who went to Penn State. I'm going into the city to have lunch with him next week."

"Thank you." His feet shifted. "I was able to talk to my dad's old boss. He'll talk to me, but he'd prefer to do it in person. He had a stroke, so can't get out much.

When I can get some time off, I'll catch the bus in and see if he has anything to help out."

Despite her warning to herself, she'd also offered to drive him into Pittsburgh.

"Do you want to ride in with me?"

Lanford narrowed his eyes, as if assessing her truthfulness.

"When are you going?"

"Monday." When she said that, she realized she'd hoped for his company all along. He'd told her Monday was his day off.

She sighed and Lanford noted it. "Anything wrong?"

She shook her head because there was nothing he could do. Nothing that was his problem. "Just a work thing."

"If you don't mind, I'll call Mr. Dawson and see if he's free on Monday." His lips tightened. "I thought investigating my case was going to be easier to do."

She grinned. "That's because you're new at this. Finding out the truth about something that happened, especially something from so long ago? That can take a lot of time, a lot of patience and often a lot of 'luck.'"

"I'm praying for something other than luck."

She was, too. But she'd learned God didn't always answer the way you wanted.

"Well, I'm heading out Monday morning. Let me know if you want to come."

"Thank you, Sheriff. I appreciate it."

Sarah found herself waiting, wanting to come up with some reason to keep talking to Lanford, and mentally slapped herself. Not what she should be doing.

She shouldn't be biased about this case. She needed to spend less time with Lanford. She'd never had this kind of problem with anyone involved in a case before and she was afraid she'd handle this all wrong. Maybe her fellow officers had been right. Maybe that last case in the city had nudged her across a line.

"Goodbye." She forced herself to return to the car and Festus. She was regretting her offer already and hoped Mr. Dawson had a busy day planned for Monday.

He didn't.

Lanford left her a note the next day.

She got the occasional note, and quite often it was… unpleasant. The older citizens of the town, and those who realized online complaints could be tracked down digitally would express their displeasure through written or printed notes. Most were signed, but some were deliberately unpleasant and anonymous. So far no one had resorted to cutting out letters from a newspaper or magazine, fortunately, but a handful of people were upset with a woman police officer. Half thought she was too harsh, half that she was too lenient. She'd received a note already this week about her lax response to the "dangerous" protests. She had a good idea who'd written that one.

Lanford's note, though, was on lined paper torn from a notebook.

> Mr. Dawson can talk to me anytime Monday. I can meet you at the station at 9, if that's okay and you're still willing to give me a lift.
> L

Nine was just fine, so she didn't need to find him to change the plan. And she refused to seek him out again.

That Sunday, she attended one of the other churches in Balsam Grove.

Monday morning she put aside her usual uniform, though that decision had nothing to do with Lanford Davies. Wearing a bit more makeup and taking time with her hair also was not related to him.

She found him standing in front of the station when she pulled up in her personal car. He waited till she'd come to a stop, then moved to the passenger door. She used her power switch to lower the window.

"Hop in."

"You don't have to do anything inside the station?"

Sarah shook her head. Lanford opened the door and slid into the passenger seat.

Sarah hadn't wanted a big vehicle for her personal use. Now she second-guessed that decision as Lanford seemed to fill the empty space. He was wearing a T-shirt and jeans again, but the clothes were clean and he'd shaven.

He probably didn't have more clothes. That didn't need to make her feel things for him.

"Do you have an address for this man you're seeing?"

Lanford lifted his hips to pull out his wallet and took out another piece of notebook paper, this one with an address written down on it. He passed it to Sarah, and she punched the address into the car's GPS.

Lanford shook his head. "I have a lot to get used to."

She cast her mind back to the technology of eighteen years ago. It had changed a lot.

She almost apologized, but it wasn't her fault and it wasn't her job to update him. They weren't friends, or anything else. She needed to remind herself.

Sarah put the car in gear and pulled out into the street. This was going to be a long two hours.

Sarah looked pretty.

He'd never seen her out of uniform before. In uniform, it was easier to think of her as the sheriff, and even though she'd said he could call her Sarah, he didn't when they were around other people. He tried not to think of her by her name when he could.

Without the uniform, she was Sarah, not Sheriff, but he was still an ex-con.

Maybe, if he could prove his innocence, he could dream about finding someone like Sarah. Someone who didn't see all his mistakes when they looked at him and was willing to take him for who he was now.

Though he wasn't completely sure who he was himself.

In any case, he could try to maintain a conversation like a normal person. He glanced around the car.

"No Festus?"

He'd never seen her without Festus hiding under her desk or in her car.

"He wouldn't be welcomed in the restaurant where I'm meeting Chad, and I can't leave him in the car in this heat. My neighbor Arthur is taking care of him for the day."

"Mr. Simpson?" The name slipped out, familiar from his high school days.

Sarah nodded. "That's right, he was your teacher."

Lanford swallowed. He could only imagine the stories Mr. Simpson would have about Lanford.

A thought popped in his head, and he spoke without pause.

"You live alone?"

As soon as the words were out, he wanted to claw them back.

"Sorry, I shouldn't have asked that. The ex-con can't ask a woman if she's living alone."

There was a lot of adjusting to this new reality.

Sarah was smiling, though, not offended.

"Lanford, there are very few secrets in this town. Everyone knows I live alone."

Not everyone. He hadn't known.

There were a few secrets, though, things not everyone was privy to. He had a couple, and there was still the big one. Who had set the fire eighteen years ago?

Sarah had stopped talking, and her smile had vanished. She must be thinking about the unexposed secrets, too.

Lanford used to be able to charm people. He'd been good at conversation. Surely, he could manage to talk for the next two hours without making things weird.

"I'm glad you have someone to keep an eye on Festus. We had a dog when I was young. Because we lived outside of town, he had the run of the property and we didn't have to worry about leaving him."

Sarah followed the new conversational gambit. "He didn't run away?"

"My mom trained him." He smiled. His mother had had a way with animals. After she died, though, his dad wouldn't allow another pet.

"Too bad she wasn't here to do something with Festus."

Lanford closed his eyes. It was too easy to imagine how much different his life would have been if his mother was still alive.

But then he wondered if she'd have been at home the night of the fire. Would there have been a fire that night if she'd lived?

It would be a hamster wheel running nonstop if he let his mind go there. He needed to get out of his own head and talk like a normal person.

"Did you have pets growing up?"

The question was lame, but it took the conversation away from his mother or anything too personal.

But Lanford wanted to ask her personal questions. Had she always been single? Why had she come to Balsam Grove from the city? Was she seeing anyone?

He couldn't ask those questions. As nice and pretty as Sarah was, she was still a cop. She was one of the good ones, he was sure, but that didn't mean her friends and coworkers were. Even if they were, they wouldn't be happy if she started dating an ex-con.

Why did he even think he had a chance with her? He'd lost his ability to charm and flirt, so that wasn't going to help him. Right now, he needed to keep all his focus on exonerating himself anyway.

It was possible she was pretending to be helping him and would take any information he gave her and use it against him. He didn't believe it, didn't want to believe it, but he was stupid if he didn't consider the possibility.

He became aware of silence in the car. He'd lost the thread of the conversation, gone into his head and missed what she'd said. He shook himself mentally and asked her to repeat it.

It was a relief when the GPS directed them off the highway. Spending too much time with Sarah wasn't good for him.

Which was unfortunate because he enjoyed her company.

"This looks like the place on the right." Sarah slowed the car to a crawl. "Number 535, right?"

Lanford nodded, noting the accessibility adjustments that had been made to the house. That added support to it being the right house.

Sarah braked. "I'll wait here while you make sure he's home."

He appreciated that she wanted to ensure someone was there to let him in. And that Lanford was welcome. He'd been surprised to be invited to the man's house.

If he wasn't invited in to the house, he wasn't sure what he'd do. He didn't expect he'd be welcome at her lunch with another cop.

He felt Sarah watching him as he climbed the steps and knocked on the door. There was a note posted, warning visitors that they needed to wait. Lanford was patient. Eventually the door was opened by a wizened man in a wheelchair.

"Lanford?" the man verified.

"Yes, sir."

"Come on in." The wheelchair backed away. Lanford opened the screen door and turned to wave at Sarah. He watched her car drive away and then stepped into the house.

"I wouldn't have recognized you. You've grown."

Lanford found the man in the chair to be a stranger, as well. His memories of Mr. Dawson were of a strong, broad figure with a booming laugh.

A lifetime away from the man in front of him.

"I didn't recognize you, either."

"Time has been kinder to you than to me. Come on in, sit."

"Thank you." Lanford chose a chair where he could watch his host.

"My grandson made some coffee, and you're welcome to help yourself. It's in that carafe. Meanwhile, you said you wanted to talk about your father. What did you want to know?"

Lanford met Dawson's eyes. He could see a trace of the former man in those eyes, intelligent and confident.

"I didn't set the fire that killed my family. I'm trying to find out who did. I hoped you could tell me if there was anyone who might have had a grudge against my father."

Chapter Eleven

Sarah arrived at the restaurant before Chad. She'd allowed extra time to drop Lanford off in case of problems, whether with traffic or directions. She found a table and ordered coffee to keep herself busy. She was reading on her phone when a loud "Sarah!" reverberated through the restaurant.

Sarah looked up with a grin. "Chad!"

"Give me a hug! I haven't seen your pretty face for ages!"

Sarah found herself squeezed in an embrace. "You know, you could come out to the country for a visit if you wanted to."

Chad sat down across from her. "Kids are keeping us busy. How are you doing in Nowhere, PA?"

Sarah always teased Chad that because of his name, he should be a WASPY New Englander, star of the rowing team and now in business with his father and grandfather. Instead, he was a Black former linebacker, who never left the city unless he had to and had been a cop since he left Penn State.

"It's quiet. I was called out to a protest, though."

He grinned at her. "Oh, yeah? Did you have to call for backup?"

"It was about a dozen high school kids with homemade signs on the lawn of their church."

His laugh boomed out again.

"That's what you have for excitement out there? Maybe I should think of transferring."

"I'm not sure the local football team is good enough for your boys. Balsam Grove is pretty quiet, so I'm not sure if I'm going to stay past this year."

"You'll always be welcomed back, Sarah."

She shrugged. Not everyone agreed. Some people thought she was too much like her grandfather.

"So, you have some information for me."

Chad let her redirect the conversation.

"Yeah, let's order, then we can get into that."

While they waited for their food, Chad caught her up on the hijinks his kids had been up to. Sarah told him about her crack police dog, Festus. Chad laughed uproariously at her description.

After their food was served, Chad brought up the topic.

"You wanted information on Riordan Davies. He died in your town, a house fire that killed his father, as well. His brother went down for that."

Sarah nodded.

"It was an open-and-shut case. Why are you looking into it now?"

"The brother just got out."

"Is he causing trouble?"

"Not yet."

Chad's eyebrows rose.

"He doesn't look like he wants any trouble. He's done

his time, doesn't want to go back. He's staying at a local church, working there. But he says he's innocent and wants to find out the truth. If he's right, someone out there might find him to be a lot of trouble."

"Sarah, prison is full of innocent men, if you listen to them talk."

"Yes, Chad, I'm aware of this." Sarah rolled her eyes. "How many of them want to prove it after they get out?"

"If they think they have a shot, and can get a big cash settlement, a few."

"That isn't what he wants, I'm reasonably confident."

"What makes you so sure?"

"There's no indication that the police made any major mistakes when they processed the case. The evidence is circumstantial, but there's no one else who fits. He's not pursuing a settlement."

"So, what's his angle?"

"He claims he was set up. Either someone was after his dad or brother, or their property, or Lanford himself."

Chad appeared to consider as he chewed. "What's he going to do if he's right and finds this mystery arsonist?"

"I plan to be there to take care of it. If someone else did this, I'll arrest them, gather the evidence and then pass it on. Same as any other case."

"Be careful. If your guy is right, someone has gotten away with murder for almost twenty years. They aren't going to be happy to be exposed now. You could find yourself in danger."

Sarah swirled a fry around on her plate. "I have to find them first. There hasn't been much to go on yet. What's up with Riordan? Any help there?"

Chad leaned back in his seat. "People still remember Dan Davies, or Riordan. I heard a lot about him. Not sure it's going to help you, though."

After getting the update on Riordan, Sarah stopped to pick up a few things at the city stores that carried products she couldn't find in Balsam Grove. It was nice to dawdle in the familiar spaces, anonymous in the city.

It was also nice to treat herself to the minor luxuries she enjoyed—her favorite bodywash, the cookies she had a weakness for.

Besides, she had time to kill. She didn't want to arrive too early to pick up Lanford.

It was midafternoon when she stopped in front of the same address where she'd dropped him off. She rolled down her window and prepared to wait for a while if necessary. She wasn't in a hurry to return to Balsam Grove. It was a nice day, and she was happy to relax, let her mind work through the problem of his case while she watched the neighborhood.

Kids were coming home from school, loud and pleased to be free. The trees were in full leaf by now, and the light was filtered through the shades of green. The noises of a family neighborhood took her back to her childhood, a happy place.

Sarah was relaxed, smiling.

After about fifteen minutes, Lanford came out the front door. The same man in the wheelchair waved him off. Lanford spotted her car in front of the house and walked quickly to meet her.

"I'm sorry. Am I late?"

Sarah shook her head. "No, I was early, and it was a nice day, so I was just enjoying it. How'd it go?"

Lanford opened the door and sat down, pulling the door shut.

"It was…good and bad. Depending on how you look at it."

"Sounds interesting. Do you want to update me on the way?"

"Sure. How was your lunch?"

Sarah moved her head from side to side. "I guess, also good and bad, depending on how you look at it."

They were soon on the highway again.

"I had a nice lunch, caught up with my friend and did some shopping. From Chad I learned that your brother was universally liked."

Lanford smiled. "He always was. He was a great guy."

"Which is good, except that we were hoping to find a reason someone set that fire. Chad found nothing to support the theory that your brother was the target. Dan didn't date a lot, and never someone else's girlfriend. He didn't cheat on tests, do drugs or step out of line at all."

Lanford shifted in his seat. "Yeah, Dan would never do that."

"There was no sign that your brother's scholarship was actively pursued by anyone else. It eventually went to a kid from Canada, but it took a while to get that settled. The track coach said no one on campus jumped on it.

"The coach also loved your brother and was very sorry about what happened."

There was silence in the car, except for the sound of tires on pavement and the movement of the air coming from the vents.

"It was always going to be a long shot, that there was anyone who wanted to hurt Dan."

"Was he a good brother, too?"

Lanford nodded. "He was great. After Mom died, Dad spaced out. We understood—Mom was really special, and we all missed her. Dan did his best to hold everything together. He wasn't a great cook, but he tried. He reminded Dad of things he was supposed to do, and anytime I wanted to talk to him, he was there.

"But he was offered that scholarship, and he had to take it. He checked with me, but I told him to go. It was hard to be at home without him, but he did a lot for me. He deserved something for himself."

Sarah was an only child, but she'd wanted a sibling. One like Riordan Davies would have been incredible.

"My neighbor, the teacher, says you got in a lot of trouble after your brother went to school."

Lanford stared at the passing scenery.

"I was a kid. My dad was gone a lot, and even when he was home, he wasn't really there. I think I was trying to get his attention. And I was angry, a lot. Angry that Mom died, that Dan left…and sometimes, so help me, I was angry at Dan. It was hard to live up to him. When he was around, that didn't bother me, but when he was gone, everyone kept telling me I wasn't like Dan.

"Being a stupid kid, I decided to do everything Dan wouldn't. Your neighbor would probably tell you I succeeded."

"He said you got in trouble, but he also said he felt badly that you were left alone so much."

"That was generous of him."

Sarah shrugged. "Maybe. Or maybe it was the truth."

* * *

It was unsettling to have your past upended over and over again. Lanford was the bad kid in town, the one everyone was glad to see the back of. He believed he'd deserved that label.

Now he was rethinking his past. Perhaps he hadn't been as alone as he'd assumed. Maybe he could have changed his path if he'd known.

That didn't help, not here and not now. The only thing he could do was discover the truth of the crime that had taken his home, his family and his freedom. That was more than enough to keep him busy, without a lot of introspection.

Still, he was glad Sarah was hearing some good things about him.

"What did Mr. Dawson have to say?"

Lanford pulled his mind out of fantasyland and returned to the practical present.

"He liked Dad."

"That's what's good and bad?"

He looked over at Sarah and shrugged. "He couldn't come up with any reason that someone would want to hurt, or kill Dad or Dan.

"He was positive Dad didn't pick up any contraband on his routes. That was one idea I had—you mentioned it, too. No one wanted to take over his routes, either. Most of the people working for him preferred to do the shorter trips."

His dad had taken those long hauls on, the ones that kept him away from home. Lanford understood that his dad had been having trouble with his mom's death, but it hurt to know his dad could have been around more, helped him. He'd chosen his own grief over his sons.

"That means there was no reason for the fire from your dad's side, either."

Lanford shook his head. He'd asked Mr. Dawson if there were any personal reasons that might be behind it. It was difficult to imagine his father involved with anyone when he gave every impression of being gutted by his wife's death, but he'd asked.

As expected, the answer had been no.

"It was nice of him to talk to you. Did you tell him why you were asking?"

"I did. I'm making an effort to be honest with everyone. He said he'd like to think that my dad's kid was a better person than an arsonist and wished me luck. He just couldn't provide any help.

"He even said, if I cleared myself, that he'd see about me getting a job."

Sarah shot him a quick glance.

"That was kind of him."

"It was. He said if I could be half as good a driver as my dad, the company would be happy to have me."

"So, a dead end, same as my talk with Chad."

"And like the storage facility."

Sarah changed lanes to pass a slow driver. She drove carefully and competently, her gaze rarely shifting from the road in front of her.

It gave him the opportunity to watch her, which he enjoyed more than he should.

She was pretty, rather than beautiful, but there was a warmth to her that Lanford found appealing. She was kind and considerate to everyone. He'd been working in the church when she'd come to check on the kids protesting. He'd tensed, prepared for something unpleasant to happen.

It hadn't.

She'd given him a chance to prove himself, and he wasn't sure, despite his intentions to be Christlike, that he would have done the same.

He wondered why she'd come to Balsam Grove. She hadn't complained about city traffic or pollution. She sounded bored with the work in Balsam Grove. Yet she was here.

It was another sign, to Lanford at least, that God was supporting him in his efforts to clear his name and find the person who'd actually set the fire eighteen years ago. Ron Harding wouldn't have helped him. In fact, at the idea he'd be proven wrong, he'd have done whatever he could to block Lanford's efforts.

She was a puzzle. A pretty, appealing puzzle.

She turned and caught him staring. He felt his cheeks heat.

"I appreciate you doing this, taking this effort for me."

"There's a good restaurant at the next exit. Want to stop for a bite?"

Chapter Twelve

Sarah had flushed when she'd found Lanford staring at her. Chad had had good cause to remind her that she had to be objective.

But Lanford's gaze had been admiring, and she hadn't responded with objectivity.

She hadn't wanted to go home and have another frozen dinner in front of the TV with Festus. She liked the idea of spending more time with Lanford. When he'd greeted her suggestion of a meal with apparent pleasure, she'd wanted to smack herself on the head. And then give herself a high five.

Instead, she was sitting across the table from him, waiting for their burgers and wondering what she was supposed to talk to him about. In spite of that, there was a bubble of pleasure generating a smile on her face.

"Thank you for your help."

Fortunately Lanford was taking all this as part of the investigation.

"No, it's fine. I'm glad to use my brain for something heavier than the crossword puzzle. I'm just sorry that we haven't made any headway."

He gave her an intense look. She wanted to know what he was thinking. She was probably better off *not* knowing.

She needed to get her mind on the case, pronto.

"We've gone through most of the obvious reasons why someone might have set the fire. I started to look for other, stranger reasons."

That intense expression on Lanford's face was gone, and she refused to admit disappointment. She still had all his attention, but now he seemed curious.

"What kind of strange reasons did you come up with?"

Their server brought their plates and offered additional pepper and drinks. When he was gone, she continued.

"I considered whether there might be another monetary reason. Maybe your father was in somebody's will, and he was killed so some other person would inherit."

Lanford swallowed his bite. "But I'm still here."

Sarah waved a hand. "I said these were strange ones. But yes, the fact that you weren't dragged back into the house to die but set up to take the blame blows that one out of the water."

A smile tugged at Lanford's lips, which was an odd way to respond to the mention of his potential death. But then, he'd already considered if he'd been meant to die. And it was no odder than the way Sarah's stomach flipped at his smile.

"That sounds like a plot out of a book."

"I'm scraping the bottom of the barrel here, so all of the ideas sound like they came from a book."

"What else?"

"A lottery ticket. Your dad or brother bought a winning ticket with someone who didn't want to share."

Lanford frowned. "I guess that's possible."

"I did some research on that. I researched lottery winners from around that time frame. I can't find any connection to your family, or Balsam Grove, or even Penn State."

"How would you ever prove that?"

Sarah shrugged. "If I had a good lead, I could try to find where the suspect was on the night of the fire. But I can't look for an alibi for everyone who won the lottery. In theory, your dad could have bought the ticket while he was on a work trip, and then it could be almost anywhere in America."

"It would have to be a big dollar amount, wouldn't it? To make it worth that much trouble?"

"Probably. Though what's worth it can vary for each person, depending on what their circumstances are and how desperate they are."

Lanford appeared to consider. "That's a good point. But would it ruin your day to know my dad didn't buy lottery tickets?"

Sarah sighed. "Of course he didn't. Why didn't he?"

Lanford shrugged. "He just never did. In any case, if he'd been going to try for a big score, it would have been when Mom was alive. After she died, he was just going through the motions."

Sarah rested her hand on Lanford's. "I'm sorry. That really sucks."

Lanford gazed at their hands. "It does."

Sarah's hand tingled where their skin touched, and she snatched it back. Desperately, she tried to move the conversation to safer channels.

"Then there's the motive writers love to put in books and movies—your dad or brother saw something they shouldn't have."

"Like, a crime?"

Sarah nodded.

"Or someone who was supposed to be dead. Or they recognized someone in witness protection."

Lanford's forehead creased.

"How would you ever know if that had happened?"

"We wouldn't. If they were killed to stop them from revealing something they saw, well, it worked."

Lanford sighed. "Maybe I'll never find out what really happened."

"I've had to get pretty far-fetched here for a reason. If you give me the name of the girl you were involved with, I might have a better lead."

Lanford's gaze shot to hers. He clenched his jaw.

"If I thought it would help, I'd ask her. But she's not in town anymore. And I don't want to spread trouble her way."

Sarah watched him, looking for any indication his resolve was wavering. There was none.

Her head said she shouldn't trust him. He wasn't being completely honest. Her heart… That was where the problems came from.

She'd wanted to help people when she chose this career. She'd believed she had.

But she'd also tried to help on that last big case before she left Pittsburgh. And that had brought about a whole lot of trouble. She'd kept a woman from being seriously hurt by an abusive spouse… But it had also kept a criminal on the street.

It was nice to help. But her job was to be a cop. She was the law.

They finished their meal in silence. Sarah didn't know what Lanford was thinking, but if her words had had any part in it, he was probably discouraged and sure he'd never clear himself.

Maybe he wouldn't. He'd need to face that possibility.

So would Sarah.

What was her endgame here? What did she think was going to happen?

If she found a motive for someone to kill Lewis or Dan Davies, and somehow, she and Lanford found evidence to support that, what then?

Lanford could get his conviction overturned. Then he'd be free to go on his way. Would he stay in Balsam Grove after he'd been cleared? Would she?

Sarah told herself she'd gone above and beyond whatever sense of duty she might have. If she got more involved with this man, even if he truly was innocent of the crime he'd been imprisoned for, she would be in the position of compromising her job, and her future in Pittsburgh.

When they got back in the car, Sarah suggested they listen to the radio and Lanford agreed. They didn't talk, and Sarah dropped Lanford off at the parsonage as the sun was setting.

Her snitch from the protest a few days ago wasn't in sight, which was a good thing. If someone asked what she'd been doing today, what would she say? She was spending the town's time and resources looking into an old case that she hadn't been asked to open again?

She'd done her due diligence. There was nothing and no one here in town that would be upset by Lanford clearing his name—at least, nothing apparent yet. And there didn't seem to be much chance Lanford was going to find something.

No one had wanted to hurt or kill his father. Or his brother. They were both admired, liked and hadn't hurt or offended anyone, outside of some random incident that no one would ever be able to prove.

The only possibility was a phone message that led nowhere.

The property was a dead end so far. Sure, it wasn't a financially successful enterprise, but people made poor business decisions all the time. That wasn't a crime. There was no fortune of oil on the land, no secrets hidden that hadn't been found when the storage facility was built.

The only possible lead was Lanford himself. He'd been a kid getting in trouble. Maybe trouble had found him.

But he hadn't done anything seriously wrong, and if he knew of anything else, he wasn't sharing it with her. Like what might have caused someone to call Dan and bring him home the night of the fire.

She reminded herself that Lanford hadn't been completely transparent. He'd put himself down as a possible motive, but he'd said he was taking care of that himself, and she had no way to make him share.

She'd done her part. It was time to close the file on her end and concentrate on the things the town paid her to do.

Like take care of Festus, the wonder police dog.

Lanford did another push-up.

He'd learned to subvert his frustration and anger into

physical activity while in prison. Like many of the guys there, he'd worked out. It wasn't always possible to use the equipment, so Lanford had learned to use his body as resistance. Push-ups, chin-ups, sit-ups—there were a lot of ways to make your muscles ache with nothing but your own body weight and time.

He dropped to the floor, chest heaving.

He pulled in air, feeding oxygen to his tired muscles. He rolled over and gazed at the ceiling.

It was warm up here in his third-floor apartment, but he was still grateful for the space. He remembered the feeling of his muscles burning after a good sprint. He used to run with Dan. Training runs. He couldn't keep up with his brother when Dan turned on the jets, but they'd done a lot of running together.

He'd missed that. Running wasn't encouraged in prison.

He wasn't in prison, not now.

He realized, if he wanted to, he could run. There was a whole range of adjustments he was making, now that he wasn't locked up anymore.

He still ate at the same times because he was used to that. Today, eating with Mr. Dawson and then with Sarah, he'd worked through a feeling of wrongness because it wasn't the right time.

It was hard to decide what to do now that he was free to do what he wanted. Freedom was scary. It was unsettling.

He pushed to his feet and pulled on a pair of shorts. He didn't bother with a shirt—it was dark, and it was hot.

His shoes weren't great for running. They didn't have a lot of shock absorption. He'd buy some better ones, but for now, he was going to run.

He raced down the steps, checking for anyone who might see him. Who might yell at him, tell him he couldn't do this.

There was no one.

He scanned his brain, remembered the stretches Dan had always done before running. Lan had laughed at him, invincible as he thought he was back then.

He did the stretches now, knowing he was far from invincible.

He stepped out the parsonage gate. There were lights on the main floor: Pastor Harold and his family. He was careful not to let the gate slam.

He turned right. It didn't matter which way he went.

His muscles weren't used to this movement, but after a couple of blocks, the motions became habit, natural. His breathing adjusted, and he was running.

Dan used to say running was a great way to think. Lanford, running solo in the dark, found his brother had been right about this, the way he had been so often.

His first night back in Balsam Grove, Lanford had listed the only reasons he could think of for why someone might set the fire and frame him for it.

After the work he and Sarah had done, they hadn't found any reasons connected to his father or Dan. It had been a long shot anyway, but it had been worth looking into.

Nothing.

The property. Sarah thought the fact that the storage place wasn't busy indicated something, but the only connection they had to those people, the ones who built and owned it, was that Billy had been Dan's best friend here in town. Billy obviously hated Lanford, but he believed Lan had killed Dan, so that made some sense.

Sarah had come up with a bunch of weird possibilities, but they were either improbable or unprovable. Lan wasn't ready to admit defeat yet.

Which meant that the only thing left was Lanford himself. Someone had either wanted to kill or hurt *him*.

A sudden pain in his calf pulled him up short. He rubbed the muscle, walking slowly and stretching it out.

He was breathing hard again and turned to head back to his temporary home.

He went through the list of people who might hate him.

He did have a list, but it was hard to imagine anyone had hated him that much. He'd been a cocky kid. He'd stolen a car, once, but it hadn't been damaged. He'd charmed the schoolteacher it belonged to and promised to do better in her class.

He and his friends had broken a couple of windows and sprayed graffiti on a few places. His dad had made him work off the repairs. They'd burned down an old shed, but that had been on his friend Randy's family property, and Randy's dad had punished Randy. Afterward, he'd learned his friends had talked about doing something bigger by burning down the Morrison barn. But he had no idea if they'd gone ahead and done it. After that night, he'd never seen those guys again.

He wondered what had happened to Randy and the others. Had someone blamed him for leading them into trouble? Maybe they'd ended up in prison, too?

No, it was hard to imagine someone had set that fire to prevent him from leading someone astray. That would be some proactive planning. And as Lanford recalled, a few of the other kids were the true leaders of their group. He'd been more of a follower.

There was one person who might have cause to hate Lanford. If that person had set the fire, he wouldn't have done it to hurt Dan or his dad—it would mean that their deaths had been totally accidental. Lanford considered it as a possibility.

Except that person had no idea what Lanford had done. Two of them had gotten into that trouble, and they were the only two who knew what they'd done. Allison would not have told, because she'd have been in as much trouble as Lanford if it came out.

He hadn't heard anything to indicate it had.

He was back at the parsonage. He went through the gate, again making sure to be quiet. The lights in the parsonage had moved to the second story, so they must be heading to bed.

For a second, the old thought patterns told him he'd be in trouble for being out late, for not being where he was supposed to be.

But he wasn't in prison anymore, and no one was going to bother him. He rounded to the stairs and went up as quietly as a cat.

He stripped down, once he was in the apartment, and used a washcloth to clean up, not wanting to run a shower when they were quiet downstairs. He switched off his lights and stretched out on his bed.

His mind continued to run. His conscience still bothered him about the one hurtful and thoughtless thing he'd done. He hadn't wanted to think about it. Had perhaps deliberately downplayed that possibility. But now he was running out of options.

And yet, to pop up now in Allison's life after all these years might blow the lid on a secret that would hurt people. If no one knew, it was better to maintain silence.

Maybe he could use one of the library computers to find out if that secret would hurt anyone if it came out.

He prayed for wisdom. And that he wouldn't cause more pain.

As he dropped off to sleep, a corner of his mind tickled. Could someone else have found out their secret…?

Chapter Thirteen

After Sarah's talk with herself, she resolved to put Lanford's case behind her and focus on her job.

She got a call about a drunk and disorderly at the Dew Drop Inn. She called for Festus and got into her car.

By the time she got to the bar, though, the drunk and disorderly's daughter had come and picked her up. To thank Sarah for responding so promptly, the proprietor offered her a free soda. Not wanting to think about the Davies case and without a lot more to do, Sarah accepted and sat on a stool to enjoy her caffeine jolt.

The jukebox was playing a country song. Apparently, the drunk woman had been mourning an old relationship and had put in a pile of coins, requesting the same song over and over. The crowd was hoping this was the last play of the song since they were more than sick of it. The only option to reset the machine was to unplug it, and it took forever to warm up again. So everyone was waiting, braced for another rendition.

Sarah took a professional glance around the establishment. It wasn't a place that would draw in a large crowd in a city with lots of competition, but here in Balsam Grove it had none. As a result, Sarah had become familiar with the place, and with the regulars. Not all required her assistance as town sheriff, but some did.

It was a quiet night. Same as most of the nights here. Sarah didn't expect to need to return once she'd enjoyed her beverage.

The bartender checked in with her. "Sorry to drag you out for nothing."

Sarah shrugged. "Not a problem. And who knows—if this song plays again someone might get violent."

He grinned and shoved some peanuts her way. She took a couple to be polite.

"Heard you went out with Lanford Davies."

Sarah almost choked on the nuts. She willed her cheeks to stay pale. She was unaccustomed to her neighbors being so familiar with her life and so interested in it.

"I didn't 'go out' with him. It wasn't a date. I had some business in the city, and since he did, as well, and didn't have a ride, I gave him one. That's all."

The bartender wiped a glass.

"He's a good-looking guy."

Sarah raised her eyebrows. "Want me to introduce you two?"

The man laughed. "No introduction is necessary. We went to school together."

Sarah wondered if it was worth asking him about Lanford.

"I know how stories fly around here, so to be clear, I'm not dating Lanford Davies, or anyone else here in Balsam Grove. Want to pass that on?"

He raised his hands. "I don't spread the stories, I just hear them. Thought you'd want to know."

Sarah sighed. "Yeah, I do. Lanford claims he's innocent and wants to find who set the fire, so I checked into a couple of things for him. If he's right, it could stir up a lot of trouble."

The man pursed his lips.

"Who else could have done it?"

Sarah noted that the man had the same problem she and Lanford did—there was no one else. He didn't immediately say Lanford had to have done it because he'd been such a troublemaking kid. Part of Sarah was still desperately looking to support Lanford's innocence, and that part latched on to even this slight hint.

"That's the problem. No one else would have wanted to harm his brother and father or set their place on fire. Unless there was a fierce battle going on for land for a storage facility."

The bartender threw his cloth over his shoulder after checking that all his customers were taken care of.

"I was at the same party as he was that night. Afterward, I racked my brains, trying to remember if Lanford was there when we talked about setting the barn on fire. We were all drinking, it was dark… I just don't know."

Sarah sat up. She hadn't considered speaking to any of the people at the party, since proving Lanford hadn't been part of the discussion at the bonfire wouldn't have changed the outcome of the case. There was no way to prove he hadn't been close enough to overhear.

"Could someone who'd talked at the party about torching the barn have set the Davies fire instead?"

She'd told herself she was done with this case, but if there was a valid lead…

He shook his head. "I doubt it. I mean, a couple of guys might have had it in for Lan. If their girlfriends had flirted with him, or stuff like that. But burning down his house? I don't think so. Everyone loved his brother, so they wouldn't have tried to go after Lan that way."

"If they didn't realize Lewis and Dan were home, though..."

"But burning down their house? That was going to hurt Dan even if he hadn't been home. I mean, you could have messed with Lan's bike. He really loved that thing. That way you'd only have hurt him. I also doubt it could have been an honest mistake. We were all drunk, but there's a big difference between an old barn and a house."

"Good point. I'm not sure Lanford will ever be able to settle this."

"Too bad Billy Robertson didn't show up at the party till later. No one liked him, so if you have to take someone down, I'd vote for him."

Sarah remembered the man who'd burst into her office, and the hate he'd had for Lanford. To be fair, he hadn't stopped by again, or called, or tried to interfere in any way.

"Would he have had a reason to do that?"

"I can't think of one. He had always been tight with Dan. But being a general pain in the behind for everyone else and working to get that storage facility built aren't enough of a reason, far as I can tell."

Sarah tensed. "Billy said he had nothing to do with the storage facility."

His brow creased. "Did he? Not what I remember."

"How exactly was he involved?"

A shrug. "I don't know. Can't remember where I got that impression."

The bartender was unconcerned, but Sarah wasn't going to let this slide. It would be the first lie she'd come across, and a lie meant someone was hiding something.

"Billy was away at school, then he got a job in the city. He didn't build U-Stor, and he didn't have the money himself to buy the property." Those were truths, as far as Sarah had been able to ascertain.

The bartender frowned. "Yeah, I'm not sure why, but I thought Billy was in on that. He was still around town that summer, I know, but I don't know what he was doing—we didn't run in the same circles. Still, doesn't prove anything."

No, no it didn't. But if Billy had been involved, then he'd lied to her. And someone lying about a detail that shouldn't matter could turn out to be something.

She finished her drink, said thanks and slid off the stool. The jukebox had moved on to another song, so the place shouldn't need her the rest of the night. She could head home, take Festus for one last walk and enjoy her evening.

And try not to chew over this inconsistency. She'd told herself she was done with the case.

One of her friends from the police academy had moved to Australia. She could send her an email to ask if it would be possible to find any information on the cousin who'd inherited the land. There. That was it. She was done.

The librarian wouldn't let Lanford use the computer unless he had a library card. To get a library card, he had to show he was a resident of the town. To prove that, she wanted a piece of mail with his name on it and the address of the parsonage as his mailing address.

He hadn't signed a rental agreement with the church, so he didn't have that for identification. He didn't have a driver's license, either. He could ask Harold if he could use the parsonage address to change his identification, but he wasn't sure how long he was staying, and he didn't want to press his advantage with the pastor. So the library was out.

He wouldn't ask Sarah for help tracking down Allison, because then he'd have to admit what he'd done. Most of the trouble he'd gotten into as a kid had been harmless. Some property damage, some vandalism. Some of it could have led to something bigger, but it hadn't, not at the time of the fire. Except for his relationship with Allison. That could have hurt a lot of people. But he still didn't believe anyone was aware of it.

If he could check on her, and she was doing well, then he hoped to keep their relationship buried as long as it had no connection to what happened that night.

Since the library and Sarah were out, he decided he'd have to ask Pastor Harold. Harold was, unsurprisingly, willing and eager to help.

"Of course you can do some research on the church computer. It hadn't even occurred to me that you might not have access to the internet. You can come in anytime and use the computer. That is, if you'd take a set of keys."

Lanford shook his head.

Harold drew a breath and frowned.

"We do have parental controls on the machine, so certain websites are not available."

It took Lanford a few minutes to understand what Harold was hinting about.

His cheeks flushed. "No, I'm not looking for pornography."

Harold's cheeks also reddened. "It's not just pornography. Gambling sites, dating websites, places where you can pirate movies and TV shows—we've blocked all of that."

Lanford drew a breath. He could tell Harold it wasn't any of his business, but the man had already helped him, and he didn't want him to worry.

"I just want to find out what happened to someone who used to live here. But I don't want everyone in town knowing I'm doing that."

Harold's whole body relaxed. "Well, that's excellent, then. If you need any help, just call me. I can be discreet."

He waved Lanford into his seat behind his desk. "I'm supposed to go to the school for a concert this afternoon, so it's all yours."

"That's very kind of you." Lanford was grateful not only for the kindness but for the confidence the man had in Lanford.

"No problem. And one moment, let me show you something."

Harold leaned around him and took the mouse, directing it to the upper right-hand corner. "You can delete your browsing history here, so no one will find out who you've been looking for."

Harold bestowed a smile upon him and left the office. Just as well. Lanford had no idea what to say to him, beyond another thank-you.

Again, Harold was proof to Lanford that God approved of his task.

The browser was open, so Lanford took a breath and then typed in a name.

It took him a while. He wasn't a good typist and had to hunt and peck his letters. As well, he didn't remember a lot about how the internet worked. They hadn't had a computer at home, and he'd missed a lot of class the last two years he was a student, so he hadn't spent a lot of time on the school's computers. There was no access in prison, and the internet worked a lot faster than it had when he'd used it previously.

After a couple of hours, he had a good handle on what had happened to Allison.

She was married to Billy Robertson. They'd been engaged at the time of the fire, and they'd gotten married soon after. That meant she hadn't talked about her affair with Lanford to Billy, or that wedding would never have happened. She'd kept the secret buried, and Lanford would do the same.

He considered. Was it a surprise that Allison and Billy had married?

She'd been the prettiest girl in town. Since Billy always liked the best of everything, it wasn't a surprise that he'd wanted Allison.

Allison's mom had raised her alone, and the family was poor. It wasn't a secret that Allison had been more interested in Billy for his money than for the rest of him, but that hadn't been a problem for Lanford.

Dan had talked to him about it once. Allison had been in his class, and they'd been friends, too. Dan had confessed that Allison had shown interest in him, but

Dan was focused on his running and doing well enough in school to get to college. He wasn't going to be distracted by a girl.

Especially not one who was dating his friend.

Dan had been torn. Billy was his friend and deserved someone who cared for him more than his money.

Allison was also his friend, and she didn't deserve Dan trying to break up her relationship. Except that Dan had thought it was the wrong one for her. He'd hinted at that once, he'd said, but she'd told him not to butt in unless he wanted to date her himself.

While Billy and Dan had gone off to college, Allison had stayed in Balsam Grove since her family had no money. Lanford hadn't paid much attention—he was saving up to get his bike at that point, and that had been his only interest.

Until Allison started coming on to him. After she and Billy got engaged, he'd gone back to school and she'd been lonely. Lanford had been lonely, too, and selfish.

After the fire, Allison had married Billy and was still married to him. Her pictures showed she was also still beautiful. She had nice clothes and a big house. For a girl who hadn't always had enough to eat growing up, he was sure she was very happy.

He wouldn't want to spend that much time with Billy, but he wished Allison well.

He closed the search browser, deleted the history and left the office. The church pianist was practicing, and Lanford let him know that he should lock up when he left.

Lanford walked around to the stairs to his own place. He felt a little lighter.

Allison was doing well, so he needed to keep her secret. Their relationship couldn't have caused the events of the night of the fire.

Now he just had to figure out what did.

Chapter Fourteen

Sarah got an email back from her contact in Australia. She had an email address for the cousin's son. Sarah hadn't used it yet.

She shouldn't spend time with Lanford. He was a good-looking man. That shouldn't be a factor, but she was afraid it was. Once in a while she caught glimpses of the charmer he must have been before he went to prison. She was liking him too much to do her job.

She was liking him too much for herself, as well. She had come to Balsam Grove for a year and then hoped to return to Pittsburgh and the force. Not to get involved with an ex-con. Even if he did find the person who had set the fire and framed him eighteen years ago, what could possibly happen between them? Why would he be the least bit interested in a cop?

But still, the loose threads niggled at her. Billy said he'd had nothing to do with the storage facility. She had no reason to disbelieve him, except for that anger he had for Lanford, which seemed more than reasonable.

He could be angry that Lanford had set the fire that

killed his friend, but Lanford had lost his brother and father. He'd suffered more, if they were comparing pain.

And it had been eighteen years. It was enough time for the edges of hurt to soften.

Then, just when she thought she could set it aside, there was what the bartender had said.

With a frustrated groan, she opened her browser on her computer. She hesitated, then sent a quick email to the son in Australia. She stated that she was a police officer and wondered if this man remembered any details of the inheritance and sale of the Davies property.

She didn't expect much of a response, if she got one at all. "I'm blaming you, Festus."

Festus's tail hit the floor a couple of times, and he sighed.

"You should be telling me to mind my own business. What kind of police dog are you?"

Seriously, that was a mystery she probably would never solve. She realized Sheriff Harding hadn't answered her last email, either. It was like he'd disappeared off the face of the earth.

She typed in U-Stor and Billy's name, to see if there were any connections between the two.

The first hit was the website for the facility. She clicked on that and looked through the website carefully, intent on any information she'd missed previously. The only link to Billy she could find was the holding company his father had owned and used for his shares of U-Stor. Now that holding company belonged to Billy, but ownership hadn't passed until his father had died.

She did another internet search and found the date of Walter Robertson's death. He and his wife had been in a fatal car accident a couple of years after the fire.

Not long after the storage facility had opened. Maybe that's why the bartender had thought that Billy was involved with it. Billy would have been very busy with all of his father's business interests at that point.

Her search of the storage facility yielded nothing further.

Then she tried typing in Billy Robertson on his own. He was a successful businessman, with a wife and son. His wife was from Balsam Grove, as well. She could ask people about this woman, Allison, but couldn't imagine there was much to follow there. Not that would relate to the arson at the Davies place, anyway.

She read the news about Billy. She scrolled back through pages of news articles until she found some from the time of his father's death. U-Stor wasn't mentioned then: it was not one of the family's biggest ventures.

She went back further, deciding to go as far as the fire. There wasn't much about Billy before his dad's death, but she found one article, just a couple months prior to the car accident.

The business magazine had interviewed Walter Robertson about the facility when it opened. The other two investors in the holding company were silent partners, and Robertson's company had purchased the land and overseen the construction.

Interesting.

The local reporter had asked about the demand for a storage facility in Balsam Grove—exactly what Sarah had wondered.

I understand what you're asking, because I had the same response when my son brought me the idea

> for the project. But the boy has to grow up sometime, so I told him we'd do it. I'd invest some of his money in it, and he could see if his idea was a good one or not.

The reporter wanted to know if his son would be involved in the day-to-day management of the project.

> He's working with me to get the thing built. Then it's up to him to take care of it. It's his opportunity to show me what he's got.

Sarah reread the comments.

The reporter hadn't added anything further relating to Billy. Not even his name. Sarah double-checked that the Robertsons only had one child. No other sons, no daughters, no illegitimate children that showed up anywhere.

Just Billy.

Sarah frowned.

Sarah had assumed, after she'd heard about Billy showing off his things, that Billy had been an indulged and spoiled child.

Walter Robertson did not sound like a doting dad. He almost sounded like he'd enjoy the project failing because it was Billy's.

It hadn't failed yet, but it wasn't exactly a resounding success story, either.

Billy had lied about his involvement in the project. Did he blame Lanford for its lack of success? Was that why he had such a strong reaction to Lanford's presence?

Sarah shook her head. That didn't make sense.

Maybe he'd wanted to save face by separating his reputation from a business that wasn't doing well, but that wasn't enough to explain the hate.

Billy might have had some cause to hate Lanford enough to want to hurt him. Maybe enough to light a fire that would destroy Lanford's home and possibly kill Lanford.

Maybe the reason also covered Lewis Davies and Riordan. Or maybe they'd been collateral damage.

And that hatred had lingered, perhaps exacerbated by Lanford surviving. So, Billy had come up with a project to destroy everything remaining about Lanford's home.

It was the best explanation Sarah could come up with that covered all the circumstances of that night. If Lanford hadn't done it, could Billy have done so?

It was the best lead she had right now. Maybe the bartender remembered more about Billy's presence at the party that night. She didn't have enough evidence to ask Billy, though.

She remembered his anger. No, he wouldn't cooperate unless he was forced to.

The bartender had mentioned Billy being at the party. She didn't remember seeing Billy's name in the reports from the case file, but she could check.

There was still the other question. The million-dollar one.

Why?

If Billy had lit the fire, it wasn't because of any information commonly known. No connection had been made at the time, and there was no talk of it now.

If there was a reason, only Billy and Lanford knew. Possibly Lanford's dad and brother had, as well. So only Billy and Lanford, who were still alive, were in that circle of knowledge.

Sarah leaned her chair back, almost poking Festus in the process.

Lanford had been cagey about who in town might have wanted to hurt or kill him. Sarah had assumed she'd be able to pick up anything serious from that time either from the old files in the station here or from talking to the people in town.

She recalled the main motives: love, money, revenge. But which one applied here?

She dropped her chair with a thud, sending Festus scurrying back to the file room.

"You've got it, Festus. We'll check through the files, and if nothing pops up, we're going to talk to Lanford. This time we have to make him open up."

Sarah hated leaving things unsettled, or unsolved. She wanted to know what happened. If her suspicions were correct, and if she took into account the hatred Billy had shown, Lanford could still be in danger.

If these files didn't reveal the mystery, then she was going to need some kind of leverage to get Lanford to talk to her. Really talk to her.

She wasn't sure she had a way to make that happen.

Lanford was working on the church's garden. After so many years locked up, he didn't mind the heat, or that some of the plants scratched him. The freedom, the pleasure of feeling the sun on his face—it all made him truly grateful for what he had.

He was surprised when Sarah parked her car on the street in front of the church. For a moment he let himself enjoy watching her.

She looked pretty, even in her uniform, with her brown hair swinging from a ponytail. She was medium height, he thought, and was fit. She walked with confidence, but not arrogance. Her expression was open, not hiding secrets.

She hadn't been to prison, or she couldn't be open like that. He hoped nothing ever happened to close up her expression, because it made him happy when he saw her.

He doubted he'd ever let himself be exposed that way again. He'd lost a lot, eighteen years ago. More than a house and family.

He knew she wasn't someone he could ever be with. Even if he proved he was innocent of the arson and resulting deaths, he had been sullied by those years in prison. In God's eyes, he was clean, but this was an imperfect world.

He'd never made plans beyond finding the real arsonist. *After* was something he hadn't considered.

But Sarah made him think of the things that had been beyond his reach since he'd been convicted. Things like a partner, a home, children.

He wasn't sure if any of that was in his future. He wondered about Sarah. Had she been married? Had she wanted a family? And he wondered again, why was she here, in Balsam Grove?

He'd been staring at her while she walked up to him. He stood from his squatting position, hands dirty with the soil clinging to the plants he'd been weeding. What had she said that he'd missed, lost in dreaming?

He shook his head.

"I'm sorry, what did you say?"

She smiled, and it warmed him inside.

"I said hello. I was wondering if we could talk."

He wasn't sure what his expression showed, but the words had made him tense.

"Nothing's wrong, Lanford, I promise. But something came up about your case."

He studied her face. She wasn't smiling as if she'd solved it and found someone else who'd confessed to it. He expected she'd look pretty pleased if that had happened.

She wasn't angry, as if she'd found more evidence against him.

Still, there was a determination in her gaze. Something was up.

He glanced at his dirty hands and rubbed the loose soil off.

"I'm kind of dirty right now."

She nodded. "Harold suggested you were able to set your own hours, so I was hoping you'd be ready to take a lunch break. I could pick up some takeout, maybe meet you at the benches behind the church?"

Some takeout behind the church sounded a lot less formal than sitting in her office. Sarah was going out of her way to help him, and he greatly appreciated it.

He nodded. "I'll clean up and meet you there. I'll bring my wallet."

She opened her mouth, and he braced for her to refuse his offer.

Instead, she nodded, and asked what he wanted from the sub shop.

It was a little thing, but it made him believe that he was free from prison in a vital way. He was earning his own way, paying for himself. He wasn't a guest of the state, and he could make his own decisions now.

There were times that overwhelmed him, but he was learning. This was his life now. He wasn't going back.

Sarah returned to her vehicle, and he found his gaze following her. Again. Fortunately, he realized what he was doing before she caught him. He walked toward the parsonage, determined to wash up thoroughly and change from his grubby clothes. There wasn't time for a shower, but he didn't want to be covered in dirt when they had their lunch together.

No, it was a meeting that just happened to fall over a meal. Still, he took time to run a comb through his hair.

Sarah was already sitting on a bench when he made his way to the back lawn of the church. There were some large old oak trees that had been there before the church was built. The oaks were the last to fully leaf, but they now provided a green canopy that protected Lanford and Sarah from the sun. Sarah had sat on one end of the bench and laid out sub sandwiches and pop in the middle. She looked up and smiled when she saw him approaching.

That smile hit him, right in the chest.

He wanted this—Sarah meeting him for lunches. Smiling up at him when he appeared. He could feel his own smile, awkward from lack of use as he answered hers.

He knew something had just happened to him, but he couldn't dwell on it. She was waiting for him to sit and join her. She wanted to talk about something.

He drew in a breath and got his expression under control. A skill he'd learned and could make happen instantaneously. He sat down, and she passed him the sandwich he'd requested.

"Thank you."

"No problem. It's nice to have an excuse to get out and eat in the sun for once."

His glance shot from the sandwich in front of him to her face.

"You have to stay in the office for lunches?"

Her lips pursed. They were bare of makeup, but the soft pink color, the shape, was distracting him. He forced himself to focus on his food.

"I guess I don't, not really. But I'm on my own, so it's easier to just stay there."

He took a bite and chewed. He considered.

"How long have you been here, in Balsam Grove?" he asked after he swallowed.

"Six months."

"You haven't made friends? Someone to meet for lunch?"

He stilled. Was that too much? Something he shouldn't ask? He shot another glance her way.

She met his gaze and shrugged.

"No, but it's my own fault." She took a bite and chewed while he waited.

"Part of it is that I'm trying to stay neutral. If something comes up, I'm not supposed to take sides, right? I'm supposed to do my job."

Lanford frowned. "But does that mean you can never have friends?"

She sighed, and he knew there was more behind that.

"I had friends back in the city, and you're right, I didn't worry about it then. But I was working for a big department, and if something came up that impacted people I knew, there were other people to take over. I could recuse myself."

He nodded slowly. That did make some sense.

"Sheriff Harding was the only law agent working here, but he had buddies. I remember that."

They'd had a poker night, the sheriff and a few others in town. And he'd been part of a fishing group.

"The other part is that I'm not sure I'm staying. So, I guess, it didn't seem like it was worth a lot of effort, not when I was probably leaving again."

"When?" As soon as the thought hit his head, the word had come out. He really wanted to know how long Sarah was going to be here.

"I signed a yearlong contract. They'll have an election after that, see if anyone will run this time. My plan was to head back to the city."

He waited, but she ate another bite of her sandwich, not offering more information. He wanted to know why, why she'd come and why she wanted to leave after a year. It couldn't be anything to do with him since this had all started six months ago.

He wanted the answers, but he'd pushed enough. He had no right to ask her to share her secrets.

"I wanted to talk to you. It's about your case."

She was changing the subject. He was both disappointed and relieved. He leaned on the relieved feeling, since the disappointment had no business happening.

He'd finished his sandwich, so he folded up the paper wrapping.

"I was called to the bar last week—the why doesn't matter. Afterward, I talked to the bartender and your name came up. He was at the party that night, the night of the fire. Billy's name came up, too, and he said that Billy was involved in the storage facility."

Lanford wondered how his name and Billy's name

had "come up." Then he processed what Sarah had said. Billy… Involved?

He frowned. That didn't match.

"After his father died?"

"No, at the beginning. When it was being developed and built."

Lanford remembered the conversation they'd had with Billy in the sheriff's office. It hadn't been that long ago, and every word had stuck. "He said he wasn't part of it."

Sarah nodded again. "I know. I did some research. And I found an article where his dad said it was all Billy's idea."

Lanford's hands were gripping the seat of the bench, hard. Had Billy found out? No, how could he? Allison would have said… Was that what she'd been trying to talk about that night? But she wouldn't have told Billy about their relationship. Not when she wanted to marry Billy so badly. How else would he have found out…?

"I also reached out to someone I know in Australia, to see if I could get more information about how the property was sold to U-Stor. Your dad's cousin, who inherited the property, died soon after. But his son remembered that his dad got the offer to purchase the land almost the same week it was deeded to him. I did some checking. Your place was not the only property available at that time, but no offer was made to the other one.

"If Billy was behind all that, as it appears, he wanted to hurt you specifically."

Lanford felt cold, despite the warm air.

"So, Lanford. I know you haven't wanted to talk about why people would have had reasons to target you. I didn't push because I could do my own research. Since you've been back, people have talked about you some, and I dug into the files at the station.

"But I didn't find anyone who'd be that upset. And I can't find any reason Billy would have wanted to harm you. But he lied about U-Stor. And he hates you, more than seems reasonable for losing a friend that long ago.

"So I have to ask you. Is there a reason Billy might have done this? Is there a reason for how he feels strongly about you? Is there any connection with the girl you had an affair with?"

Lanford tilted his head back, looking up into the branches of the oak tree. He didn't want to believe it, but he had to consider the possibility that Billy had found out about his relationship with Allison.

The guilt hit, hard. If Billy had done this, he'd set the fire because of Lanford's selfish actions.

He'd murdered his father and brother as surely as if he'd lit the match himself.

Chapter Fifteen

Sarah saw comprehension dawn on Lanford. There *was* something to do with Billy, Lanford knew it, and the guilt was overwhelming.

She wanted to reach over, touch him, assure him everything was all right. But they didn't have that kind of relationship, and she didn't know if everything *was* all right. He'd deliberately kept this knowledge from her. And she was very afraid that whatever it was might not be over and done with.

"Can you tell me what it is, Lanford?" She spoke softly, encouragingly. Was his life in danger? Was hers?

He opened his eyes, but was gazing upward, at the tree overhead.

"It's not just my secret. It could hurt someone else."

Sarah felt that one. It struck close to home. *It must be the girl.*

She understood the desire to protect someone, but also the need to solve a case—and how difficult a choice it could be when those two things were in opposition.

It was a choice she'd made, perhaps wrongly.

It also meant that there was, perhaps, something she could do to convince Lanford to trust her.

She could share with him the information she'd been guarding. Why she was in Balsam Grove. The real reason, not that she just needed a break.

"Can I tell you a story?"

Lanford dropped his head and turned to her. She could see the wariness in his eyes. He expected the full-court press.

What she wanted to do was expose a little of herself, the part of her that had made wrong choices. She could show him that she also made mistakes. Then he might not be afraid to trust her with his.

"This story is about a cop in the city, before she moved to a small town for a year to get herself straightened out."

She saw him cock his head, the understanding on his face. The surprise.

She leaned back on the bench and stared up into the branches he'd been looking at so attentively.

"She became a cop because she wanted to help people, like her dad and granddad before her. It was a family tradition, and as an only child, she was the only one who could carry it on. But there was a twist to this story.

"Not long after her dad became a cop, her grandfather was arrested. Turned out, he'd been on the mob's payroll, giving them information.

"Her father was clean, but he spent his whole career making up for the mistake her grandfather had made. This woman has been fighting that same battle.

"She did her job for years and did it well. Then came one particular case."

She could feel Lanford's attention focused on her.

"There are some very unpleasant people in this world. People who will hurt others for their own gain and amusement. The police department was after one of those people. He broke the law, but he was very careful. The department was using a lot of resources to build a case against him.

"They found an informant—the wife of the bad guy. He was abusive so she was willing to give information on him and wanted to be extracted when they finally took him down. She went to the same nail salon regularly and would pass over information there.

"Then one night he beat her especially badly. Badly enough that she had to go to the hospital."

She saw the jerk Lanford gave out of the corner of her eye. The story wasn't going to get any better.

"This cop met the wife in the hospital. She'd been told by her commanding officer that they almost had the case finished against this woman's husband. But they needed the wife to go back, get some more information for them.

"The wife was petrified to go home. She was sure that next time, he'd kill her."

Sarah swallowed. She couldn't be objective about this. She was pretty sure now that she never would. How was that going to affect her career plans going forward?

"The wife begged the cop to help her escape. The cop had been to quite a few domestic violence calls. She believed the woman.

"She knew the risk she took in helping the victim. Some would suspect she was following in her grandfather's footsteps. It was a tough call, but she took the woman back to her home to collect her dog. Then the cop took her to a shelter."

Sarah had taken this year away from the city to try to understand her decision and see if she would have changed it in a similar circumstance. She still hadn't figured that out. But she knew she'd brought down a lot of suspicion on herself.

"The woman was safe. But the case was blown up. The man fled, and that was that. Months of work, gone."

Lanford spoke. "You did the right thing."

The words warmed her, but she continued with her narrative.

"There weren't any specific consequences for the cop. None of her fellow officers said it was wrong, but there was always the worry that she was dirty. And she was well aware more people would be hurt by this criminal and his victims wouldn't get justice. Other criminals would be encouraged by the department's failure."

Sarah unclenched her hands.

"There was nothing specific, but the cop began to feel unwelcome at get-togethers, ignored at work. She still had friends on the force, but she decided to take a break. She took a posting in a small town for a year.

"She hoped to work things through and see what she might have done differently. To be squeaky clean for a year, and try to look for the big picture."

She paused.

"How's that going?"

She shook her head. "I'm not good at removing my feelings. I care about the people I want to help. Everyone tells me I'm not clergy and I'm not social services…so maybe I'm not in the right place. Maybe I'm not really cut out to be a cop."

Lanford reached out a hand, touched her arm. She turned to him.

"No, I think you're needed as a cop. I heard a lot of stories while I was in prison. I didn't have it so bad—the sheriff here wasn't abusive. He might have been lazy and not worked very hard to find another solution to the arson, but I can't fault him for that when we haven't been able to find one, either.

"But other guys, other stories. They could have used someone who would have cared. That's never a problem."

Sarah gave him a smile, one a little shaky around the edges.

"Thank you. I appreciate you saying that. Maybe what I need to do is work a little harder for what I believe in. Since I'm a woman, I get the 'emotional' label a lot."

Lanford gripped her arm a little tighter.

"I appreciate the work you've done to help me. Even if that's what's gotten you into trouble in the past, I'd still say being emotional is a good thing. But it probably isn't easy."

Sarah sniffed.

"Yeah, there's that emotion. Thank you, Lanford. I needed to hear that."

"From an ex-con?" His voice was wry.

"Maybe especially from an ex-con. We, as cops, are supposed to serve and protect. It doesn't say we can exclude ex-cons from that. Or anyone."

There was a moment of silence. It was comfortable. Sarah eased her mind, putting Lanford's comments into the mental file she had as a database for the decisions she had to make this year.

She'd almost forgotten why she'd asked to talk to Lanford when he spoke.

"It was about a girl."

* * *

Lanford hadn't meant to share this with Sarah. She already knew so many of the ways he'd messed up.

It was stupid to want to impress her. She was a cop. He had spent eighteen years in prison and might never be able to prove he hadn't set the fire that took the lives of his dad and brother.

But it was important to him to give her the truth because he liked her, a lot. He liked that she was smart, but also caring. That she'd given him a chance. That she'd risk her own reputation for someone else. She'd tried to help him and never appeared to judge him.

She'd be judging him now.

The only way they were going to find answers, though, was if he was honest. If he wanted to prove that he'd been innocent of the arson and murder charges, he was going to have to confess to what he had been guilty of.

He'd been seventeen. Of course it had been about a girl.

"Allison Kelly was beautiful."

Sarah reacted. She recognized the name. Lanford continued, determined to push through before he lost his nerve.

"Her family was also poor. There was her and her mother and a couple of younger sisters. We weren't exactly rich, not like Billy and his family, but I'm pretty sure Allison's family didn't always get enough to eat.

"She was Dan's friend, so I always knew of her, but I was a little late getting into girls. By the time I was paying attention, she was engaged to Billy.

"Everyone assumed she was mostly interested in Billy because of his money. He wasn't the best-looking or the fittest guy in school, but he had stuff, and he had money, and he was happy to spend it on her."

Sarah made a movement, and he turned to see her watching him.

"I don't mean that to sound judgmental. I didn't blame her, and I don't think Dan did, either.

"Well, to make this long story short, Billy went off to college, as did Dan. Allison stayed behind, no money for school, and she was still officially dating Billy. But she was bored, I guess.

"She started to spend time with me. I was lonely, with Dan gone and Dad out on the road so much, so we were together a lot. When Billy came back on breaks from school, she ignored me, but I was okay with that. We were just messing around and I was spending my time getting in trouble and hanging out with the kids who liked trouble.

"The Christmas before the fire, Billy proposed to Allison. I was surprised, always thought Billy would find someone 'better' at school, but he proposed, she said yes and had a big ring. Dan was worried that she'd agreed for the wrong reasons, but I told him to mind his own business. Not sure if my argument was the reason, but he didn't say anything."

Lanford rubbed his hands on his pants. It was hard to confess this, but if Billy had found out, it might be enough reason for him to have set the fire.

"I teased Allison about being engaged, and how we couldn't hang out anymore. She said she needed a bit of fun before she settled down. And we…well, we did more than we should have."

"You slept with her?"

Lanford nodded, eyes on the ground.

"We were careful, and no one found out. Partly because I was so often hanging out with guys getting into trouble. If I wasn't with them, they thought I was at home. No one was at my place to tell on me. Not sure what Allison told people, but most of the time I had the house to myself, and we took advantage of it."

Sarah was putting the pieces together.

"That's who you were with at the party, when the others were talking about setting a fire—Allison."

He nodded, still not looking at her.

"Yeah. I don't remember a lot, because I'd been drinking. Dan and Dad had set off on a long delivery together, and I was feeling sorry for myself. Drank a lot. I didn't expect to see Allison that night—she didn't normally come to that kind of party.

"She showed up and gave me a nod, so I followed her off into the bushes. She said she needed to talk to me about something.

"I didn't want to talk. I was afraid she wanted to get serious, maybe break up with Billy. So instead of talking, I tried to take off her clothes.

"She shoved me away, said something about later. I fell over when she shoved me, so I didn't see where she went, but she must have gone home.

"I didn't see her again. I can't imagine Allison would have told Billy about us, and no one else knew.

"I looked her up on the church computer. She's married to Billy, and they have at least one kid. So, he couldn't have found out, right?"

He glanced at Sarah then, needing to read her expression, even if it was going to hurt him.

He didn't detect judgment in her eyes, or disdain.

"Lanford, people do very strange things. I don't

think you should make assumptions. We need to talk to Allison."

"I'm not sure she'd want to talk to me. She was a friend of Dan's, too, and would blame me for his death, just like Billy. And I'm positive I'm part of a past she doesn't want to revisit."

Sarah looked away, mouth quirked as she thought.

"I'll call her and ask if I can talk to her. She doesn't know me. I'll try to set up a time when Billy isn't around, because you're right… If your secret is truly safe, we don't want to upset her life. But if Billy did learn of your relationship, then he's the first person we've found with a legitimate motive.

"There's nothing in the file to indicate whether he was ever interviewed at the time."

"He must have been in town."

Sarah's head tilted.

"Dan was home from school, so Billy would have been, too. I don't remember seeing Billy then, so maybe I'm wrong."

"The bartender I spoke to said that Billy was at the party."

"Was he? I don't remember him being there, but it's possible. I was pretty drunk, and he did often come back."

"To see Allison."

He felt the heat in his cheeks.

Sure, he'd been a seventeen-year-old kid. But he'd known that what they were doing was wrong. They both had.

He'd only been thinking about himself, the pleasure, the idea of getting one over on Billy, the rich kid no one liked, no one but Dan.

Dan would have been so disappointed with him.

"This couldn't be what your brother left a message about, could it?"

It was like Sarah was reading his mind.

"I hope not. He'd have been upset. But I'm not sure he'd consider it enough to ruin my life. It was bad, but the other stuff I was doing was just as bad."

"Is there any reason Allison would have confided in your brother?"

Allison had liked Dan. He was pretty sure that if Dan had shown interest in Allison, Allison would have dropped Billy. Dan was a smart guy, and he wasn't just running track at college. He was getting a degree. He'd have been able to get Allison out of this little town.

But Dan wouldn't have touched Allison, not when she was Billy's girl.

Unlike Lanford.

If Allison had had a problem, a big one, she might have talked to Dan. If it was something she couldn't tell Billy. And Dan would have tried to help.

Lanford sighed.

"She might have talked to him if she had a problem, but she wouldn't have mentioned she was fooling around with me for no reason. He'd have been upset with both of us. She liked him—she wouldn't have wanted to confess something bad about herself."

He gathered up the debris from their lunch, carefully putting everything back in the bag it had arrived in. Sarah was staring forward, eyes narrowed, her brain obviously working.

"You're right, the thing with Allison might be nothing. But it's worth checking out. Let me look into it."

Lanford stood, ready to toss the garbage and get back to work. One thing he wasn't messing up.

"Lanford." Sarah's voice was insistent.

He met her gaze.

"Don't do anything without me, okay?"

He shrugged. "I have no vehicle, so I think it's safe to say I won't be doing anything without you. I won't call her. I'll wait."

"Thank you. Thank you for sharing and thank you for trusting me. I'll be careful with this information, I promise."

"I know." He did. He trusted Sarah. Trusted her… And more.

Chapter Sixteen

Sarah put down a bowl of water for Festus and then sat at her desk.

There were no messages for her. Balsam Grove had been enjoying a quiet stretch. She had her own theories about why, including the phase of the moon, and the fact that the high school was approaching final exams. The weather was turning warm, but not yet hot enough to shorten people's tempers. She'd been called out to an automobile accident last night, but that was the biggest thing that had happened for days.

Fortunately, no one had been hurt. The car required a tow, but it would also survive.

She leaned back in her chair and rested her heels on the desk. Then she dropped them to the floor again. The position was not comfortable, despite what she always saw in movies.

Festus finished his drink and slipped into the space under her desk.

It was time for her to figure out the next step in Lanford's case.

He was sure that Billy couldn't know what had happened between Allison and him all those years ago. Sarah was equally confident Lanford was wrong.

The slight evidence they'd found, if you could even call it evidence, indicated that Billy had been involved in the U-Stor development and lied about it, and that Billy hated Lanford. She'd quizzed her neighbor Arthur about Billy and Lanford, but he knew nothing, except that Dan and Billy had been friends, and Dan and Lanford were brothers. Nothing to explain the hatred the other man had for Lanford.

Discovering that his girlfriend, no, fiancée was cheating on him would have been painful. Some men would break off the relationship and move on, story over. But for some men, that wasn't enough.

She'd like to talk to the people who'd been at the party that fateful night. No one had interviewed Billy, and as far as she knew, no one had seen him at the party, except the bartender. But then, no one had mentioned Allison, either.

If she allowed that Billy had gone to the party, been on the outskirts unnoticed—after all, it had been after dark, outside, not impossible for someone to be unremarked, as Allison was—he might have seen Allison with Lanford.

What if Billy had? And decided to get revenge on Lanford by setting the fire?

It made perfect sense. Especially if he hadn't realized his best friend had come home.

But, if she was playing devil's advocate, why had Billy married Allison afterward? Had she apologized sufficiently? Was he embarrassed for anyone to know she'd cheated on him?

If so, why had Allison never mentioned anything?

Had she figured it out and blackmailed Billy into staying with her?

If that was the case, would she ever admit the truth?

Sarah decided then that she wouldn't give Allison a heads-up about her visit. She wanted to catch the woman off guard. If this was the truth, then without testimony from Allison, there was unlikely to be enough evidence to clear Lanford. Though perhaps knowing the truth would be enough for him.

Would Billy still want to kill Lanford?

Sarah stood up, restless. Festus whimpered as her foot nudged him. Sarah went to the tiny fridge and pulled out some water. She reminded herself that all the evidence wasn't in, and she was merely speculating.

There were other things to consider. Dan's phone call to Lanford. That had happened while Lanford was at the party. If Billy had seen Lanford and Allison there, and in a burst of hatred and jealousy set the fire, then the call from Dan was an unconnected detail.

She didn't like loose threads.

Had Dan also found out about the romance? As Lanford himself had pointed out, that wasn't the kind of thing that would ruin Lanford's life. Not unless Dan thought his friend Billy would kill over it. Could Dan have been friends with a man he believed could be a killer? Would he have withheld telling his friend that he was being used if he believed he was that kind of man?

Then there was the thing Allison had wanted to discuss with Lanford, the reason she'd gone to the party at all, as far as anyone knew.

Had she wanted to break things off with Billy and start a committed relationship with Lanford? Had Dan been aware of her plans and feared it would ruin Lanford's life?

That led back to Dan believing Billy was vindictive and violent enough that he wouldn't just walk away from a broken relationship. It would also mean Dan thought Lanford was interested in a serious relationship with Allison.

Perhaps Lanford had lied to Sarah about how he felt about Allison, but she doubted it. He'd been embarrassed to recount the story, and if he'd been in love with the girl, he would have painted it as a romantic tale of star-crossed lovers.

As well, nothing in the files on Lanford, or the stories around town indicated he was serious relationship material.

He'd been trouble. Selfish, heedless, seeking attention. That made sense with a history of abandonment: his mother died, his father retreated and his brother went away to school. If he was getting his emotional needs met in a relationship, he'd have been less of a troublemaker.

There was always the possibility that Lanford was correct, and that Billy had never known about the affair.

No, she didn't think that was right.

She'd seen the way Billy had looked at Lanford. Plus, Billy had lied about the storage facility.

Billy had come back to Balsam Grove because Lanford had returned. Billy's feelings about Lanford were strong, negative and very personal.

Her instincts told her Billy had found out.

There was one other twist, something that she'd considered that Lanford apparently had not. If you were sexually active with a woman, and she wanted to talk, there was always the possibility of a pregnancy.

Lanford had said they were careful, but accidents did happen. And if Allison had been pregnant and wanted to talk to Lanford, how would that have played out?

This was speculation, because there was no evidence of a baby. In fact, Sarah had done the research, and Billy and Allison had adopted a child soon after they married. There were no other children, biological or adopted.

She'd found an interview where the couple mentioned that a friend had had a baby, no father in the picture, and they'd decided to use their financially and emotionally stable circumstances to take care of the child.

If Allison had found herself pregnant, couldn't she have passed the child off as Billy's? If for some reason it couldn't have been Billy's, wouldn't that have ended the relationship between the two of them? Could Billy have pressured her to have an abortion and then married her? Why? Why stay with her?

If Allison had been pregnant with Lanford's baby, maybe Billy had been enraged enough to start a fire at Lanford's house. But how would he have found out about the baby, and when? And why would he stay with Allison?

It might explain Dan's call, too, since becoming a father at seventeen might be described as ruining a man's life. But how would Dan have known? Would Allison have talked to him about it? Would he have called Billy?

Did Allison have something over Billy's head that she could blackmail him into staying with her? And if any of this had played out, why had Allison kept quiet?

Or maybe Allison had set the fire. To keep Lanford

quiet. Was she that determined to marry Billy and gain the security that could only come from his money? Was there any reason she might believe Lanford would reveal her secret? Maybe if she'd been pregnant, she was afraid Lanford would want to claim the child.

Sarah dropped down again at her desk, fingers massaging her temples.

She could speculate and spin stories till the cows came home, but it wasn't going to get them anywhere.

Allison was the hinge. Sarah had to talk to Allison.

Sarah wiggled the mouse to bring her computer back to life.

Billy was due to participate in a charity golf tournament in a couple of days. It was a locals-only event, not attracting celebrities.

Allison might attend to watch him, but she also might be at home. Sarah could take a drive to their home, check out the neighborhood and knock on the door.

Sarah wouldn't take her work vehicle or wear her uniform. If the other woman answered the door, Sarah would tell Allison she had questions for her, related to Balsam Grove.

Would it be enough to get Allison to talk to her?

She tapped the desk with her finger, and Festus whimpered.

Then she thought of a plan that would catch Allison off guard, and surprise her enough to possibly get her to reveal the truth.

She'd drive up with Lanford.

If the thing between Allison and Lanford had been more than a high school fling, that might be enough to unbalance her and get her to talk.

Allison might find it easy to refuse Sarah, a woman

she didn't know. It would be more difficult to refuse your former lover, a man just out of prison.

Sarah reviewed the commitments she had over the next week. Lanford had said he didn't work on Sundays and Mondays.

She didn't want to wait that long. Something inside her was pushing her to move. If there was any possibility that Billy or Allison had done this, they might decide to try again.

Lanford hadn't been surprised when Harold tracked him to the basement of the church to talk to him. The pastor was friendly and concerned, going well beyond the requirement for his position. It was obvious Pastor Harold was concerned for Lanford, not over what Lanford might do. If he had questions, Lanford was happy to answer them.

However, Pastor Harold was just passing on a message. Sarah had called to ask if Lanford could take a day off to go with her on a police matter, a day that didn't align with his usual Mondays off. Pastor Harold had quickly agreed, as anyone would have predicted.

That was how Lanford found himself again traveling in Sarah's personal car, headed back toward Pittsburgh. Lanford was wearing the same clothes as last time. His wardrobe was limited, and he wasn't ready to invest what money he had available in more.

Sarah was distractingly pretty in a sundress and sandals. She looked as unlike a cop as she had since he'd known her.

He hadn't been out with a girl for eighteen years. He'd never had a girlfriend. But he realized what he was feeling for Sarah was special.

And useless.

He focused on her plan instead.

"You're positive Allison won't be going to the golf club?"

Lanford didn't know anything about golf clubs. He'd never been a member before he went to prison, and it wasn't an option for prisoners. His only exposure was through movies. He couldn't remember much about that part of any movies he'd watched, either.

"If I'm wrong, then we'll come back."

"It wouldn't be better to check first?"

Sarah shot him a glance and then returned her attention to the road.

"I thought it would be a little strange to call up and ask her if she was going to stay home."

"Yeah, but you're a cop. Can't you find out things?"

"Tracking regular people isn't something we normally do. I have no reason to ask a judge for a warrant. I don't have a superpower to find out otherwise."

"You really think it's this urgent?"

Sarah signaled and pulled out into the passing lane to go by a slow-moving truck.

"I don't know. But if Billy did find out about you and Allison, and there were some circumstances around that that drove him to set the fire, he might have done it to hurt you. Physically. He might have wanted to kill you. And if that's the case, he might try again."

Lanford frowned.

"It just doesn't fit with the guy I knew."

"I saw him in the station. He hates you."

"That's because Dan was his friend and he blames me for the fire."

"Was he that close a friend of Dan's? It's been almost two decades, and you've been in prison for all those years. It would have to be a very close friendship to incite that much hatred."

"I don't know. I assumed this would be easier, less confusing."

"If Billy did commit this crime eighteen years ago, he has a lot to lose. Or, another option is that Allison might have set the fire to protect her relationship with Billy."

Lanford had never considered that. It didn't make sense to him. He'd never been a threat to Allison. Could she have thought he was?

"Oh, Festus!"

Sarah held a hand to her nose. It hit Lanford then. He looked over his shoulder into the back seat where Festus was lying soundly asleep. There was no mistaking the source of the smell, though. Festus had digestive issues this afternoon.

"Couldn't find a babysitter for him?"

Sarah's face was still scrunched up. "No, my neighbor is out today. Maybe Festus *does* have the ability to convince a witness to talk."

Lanford's lips twitched. "As in, if they refuse to confess you could hit them with one of his stink bombs?"

Sarah snorted, and her hand moved from her nose to cover her mouth. Her cheeks flushed.

It seemed Sarah was embarrassed by her laugh. She needn't be. Lanford found it charming.

He found everything about Sarah charming. She was a danger to his peace of mind.

Billy had a large, showy home. It was in a gated community, but Sarah had brought her badge and that got them through the gates. The grounds were immaculately maintained. Nothing was out of place. After spending the last weeks working on the church gardens, Lanford knew exactly what kind of effort that required.

Billy was doing well financially, at least.

After a moment of staring at the door of the house, the two of them unwilling to exit the car, Sarah reached for her door pull.

There were no vehicles in the driveway.

"She may not be home, or her car may be in the garage. Only one way to find out."

Lanford was reluctant to move. It had been years, but when he'd last seen Allison, he'd been someone. A troublemaker, true, but he had been in control of his future, as he thought. He'd been confident, independent… Free.

Now he was the guy who'd been in prison for eighteen years. He wondered if she'd regard him with disgust. He wondered if she might have been the one to set the fire.

He forced himself out of the car. Sarah was opening the back door, dragging Festus out.

Lanford looked at the house doubtfully.

Sarah shrugged. "I can't leave him in the car—it's too hot."

Sarah led the way up the sidewalk, Festus and Lanford following reluctantly. At the door, Sarah drew in a breath and pressed the bell. Lanford braced himself. He wondered if Allison would recognize him.

They heard footsteps approaching the other side of the door. They were heavier than Lanford would have expected, and he wondered if Sarah's information had been at fault. Maybe something had happened, and Billy hadn't gone to play golf. Maybe his angry visage was what they'd see.

The door pulled open, but it wasn't Allison or Billy who stood there. It was a kid, a teenager. He stood almost as tall as Lanford. He had dark hair and clear gray eyes. The jolt of recognition almost hurt.

It was as if someone had taken seventeen-year-old Lanford and time-traveled him to the current day.

Lanford stopped breathing. His brain shut down. He could do nothing but stare in shock at this younger version of himself.

Lighter footsteps tripped down the hallway toward them.

"Ri, how often do I tell you not to open the door until—"

Allison, an older, more polished and brittle Allison, appeared behind the boy. She looked at Sarah, and a puzzled expression crossed her face. Then her gaze landed on Lanford.

She turned white. "No..."

Chapter Seventeen

Sarah didn't need any special training to start putting the puzzle pieces together. There were still questions, but there was no doubt who this boy was.

Lanford's son.

Allison had wanted to tell Lanford that she was pregnant at the party.

A glance at Lanford beside her showed him frozen in shock. Allison was still white and had a hand on the hallway wall to support herself. The boy, Ri, was also looking confused.

"Allison Robertson? I'm Sarah Winfrey, the sheriff from Balsam Grove. I was hoping to talk to you."

Allison tore her gaze back to Sarah.

"Um, yes, of course, uh..."

"Do you mind if my dog comes in? It's too hot to leave him in the car."

Allison's gaze sharpened as her mind began to function again.

"Ri, why don't you take the dog for a walk? If it's been in the car all the way from Balsam Grove, it would like some exercise. I need to talk to these people."

The boy's chin jutted out.

"I was supposed to—"

"If you want to drive your car anywhere this next month, then you'll take the dog and go for a walk. Now."

The boy glared at his mom. She held his gaze. His expression turned sulky and then he shrugged.

"Whatever."

Sarah held out the end of the leash, and the boy took it with barely a glance at her. His attention was on Lanford. Lanford was still standing as if frozen.

"Come on in." Allison stood aside, anxious to get them in the house.

Sarah could understand why.

Sarah took Lanford's arm and pushed him forward. She closed the door behind her, with a last glance down the sidewalk.

The boy was dragging Festus along, eyes still on his own front door.

"This way."

Allison led them to a great room with an expansive kitchen on one side and a comfortable sitting room on the other. She kept shooting glances at Lanford, then glancing away. Lanford wasn't looking at either of them.

"Have a seat. Can I get you a drink? Iced tea? Water? Beer?"

Lanford shook his head. Sarah sat on a couch and he joined her.

"Just water would be lovely."

Allison opened a cupboard to bring down glasses, busying herself with ice and water, using the activity to pull herself together.

By the time she brought them their drinks, she almost resembled the composed woman Sarah had seen in the photos online.

"How can I help you?"

Her voice was polite, in control. But there was a nervous tic near her jaw, and her gaze kept flitting over Lanford and leaving again.

"I met your husband briefly at the sheriff's office in Balsam Grove. He was upset when he saw Lanford. I've been looking into the arson case from eighteen years ago, and I had a few questions—"

"What did you call him?" Lanford broke in.

She could hear the tension in his voice. Allison turned to Lanford and wasn't even pretending any longer to care what Sarah was saying.

"We called him Riordan. Ri for short."

Lanford swallowed. "What did you do?"

Allison tried to bluster. "I don't know what you're talking about."

"Is it why you wanted to talk at the party? Before—before the fire?"

Allison opened her mouth and then closed it, staring at the ceiling.

"I tried to tell you. You were too drunk to listen."

Lanford was having an out-of-body experience. He could see the three of them in that room, but from above. Nothing was real.

Then Allison's words hit him, bringing him down to earth. The impact was painful.

He'd been drunk and she hadn't told him she was pregnant… So she'd confessed to someone else.

"Did Dan know? Was that why he called? Is that why he and Dad cut their trip short?"

He wanted her to say no. He needed her to say no. But of course she nodded.

Allison's eyelashes fluttered, and she reached a finger beneath her eyes to wipe away the moisture.

"I didn't know what to do. Billy was going to flip. I had no idea how you were going to respond. So I called Dan. He said he'd help, that he'd talk to Billy. And to you.

"I didn't want to tell you. I mean, it wasn't like we were going to get married and live happily ever after. But this was your mess, too. I thought Dan could make things work somehow."

If anyone could have, it would have been Dan. But he finally understood what Dan had meant in that last message, the one Lanford hadn't heard till after Dan was dead.

This was definitely a life-altering thing. It would have messed up his future. That was, if there hadn't been the fire, and he hadn't ruined his future with eighteen years in prison.

He narrowed his gaze. "Billy. When did he find out?"

Allison was twisting her hands in her lap, refusing to meet his gaze.

"At the party. After I left you, I was going to head home and wait for Dan. But Billy was there.

"I'd told him I wasn't feeling good and was staying home that night. He didn't believe me, I guess. He'd followed me to the party and saw us together."

His own memories of that night were blurry, but he remembered kissing Allison, running his hands under her T-shirt, trying to pull it off.

If Billy had been watching, he'd have known exactly what the two of them had been doing while he'd been at school.

Lanford's guilt weighed down on him, but he fought it back. He'd pay for this, later. Right now, he needed to know what had happened that night.

"I told him I was so sorry, that it didn't mean anything, it had just happened. I promised him that no one knew, and I'd stop and could he forgive me…

"He was so quiet. He just dragged me back to the car. I wasn't totally lying. The morning sickness was brutal. I had to stop on the way to his car so I could be sick in a bush."

"He asked if I was drunk. And I just laughed. I mean, I couldn't drink anything if I was pregnant, right?

"He slapped me. He'd never… I was shocked. And I said, 'I'm pregnant.'"

He'd slapped her?

"What did he say?"

Allison met his eyes for a brief moment, then her gaze skittered away again.

"He didn't say anything. He took me home. Told me to wait.

"That's what I did. I thought maybe Dan would call."

Lanford noticed that his fists were clenched, his knuckles white.

"What did Billy do?"

She swallowed. "He came back later. He said you weren't going to be able to help me with anything—you would be sent to prison. And I was going away till I had the baby."

Lanford pushed himself to his feet.

"And you didn't say anything? After the fire?"

Allison shrank into her seat and he forced himself to step back. Forced that burning anger down.

"I couldn't, not then. He drove me to his family's summer place. Took my phone and ripped out the phone line there.

"He said he could get my mom fired if I didn't stay put. That she'd never find another job and my sisters would starve. That he'd ruin my family's life, tell them I was a whore—"

Sarah flinched at that.

"I was tired, and frightened. And I didn't know about the fire, not for a long time."

"Billy came back, about a week later. He said we were getting married. I asked about the baby... He said we'd pretend to adopt it. His dad had connections. He could make everything work, or he could destroy me and my family."

Lanford couldn't look at Sarah. He didn't want to see her face. But now she broke into Allison's recital.

"Why would Billy adopt Lanford's child? Did you talk him into it?"

Allison shook her head.

"Billy can't have children. He hadn't bothered to tell me until then. He got the mumps one summer and it left him sterile. It's rare, but it does happen.

"He told his parents that Lanford had slept with a girl in the next town and got her pregnant. And we were adopting the baby because Billy wanted to respect Dan. We called him Riordan. Ri knows he's adopted, but he doesn't know I'm his mother.

"Or anything about his father."

Lanford found himself pacing the room, his brain scrambling to make sense of what Allison was revealing. His mind kept coming back to the boy he'd met earlier in the doorway.

Riordan. His son.

He stopped by the fireplace, leaned a hand on the mantel, struggled to get his temper under control.

Why, God?

If only he hadn't been so drunk that night. If only Allison hadn't called Dan. If only he hadn't messed around with her…

He drew in a long breath, shot up a prayer.

He turned back to Allison.

"Billy set the fire, then? Or was that you? Did you want to kill Dan?"

Allison's lip trembled.

"It wasn't me. I didn't ask Billy what happened. I didn't want to know. I should have done things differently—I understand that now, but I was trying to protect my family. My son."

My son. Lanford had the same claim.

Sarah asked Allison for more details. Lanford stopped listening. He needed to deal with the information he already had.

Billy had set the fire. He'd done it to hurt or kill Lanford. It was his fault.

That pain shot deep. He'd always feared this. That somehow, even if he hadn't lit the fire, hadn't spread the gasoline, he'd been the one responsible.

He drew in a shuddering breath.

There was nothing he could do now. It was over. Done.

Finished.

He remembered the last moments of Jesus. "It is

finished!" he'd said. Then he bowed his head and gave up his spirit.

He'd also said, "Father, forgive them; for they know not what they do."

Imagine forgiving someone like that. Could he forgive himself? *You're forgiven.*

The words echoed in his head, and he looked around, almost suspecting someone had spoken them.

Only Sarah and Allison were in the room with him.

But some of the weight slid off his shoulders.

Yes, he had more to be forgiven for. But God had promised to forgive it all. It was going to take Lanford some time to accept that, but he knew it was a truth. It was hard to come to terms with it, but he'd suspected it ever since the fire.

It was his fault.

But now he had something else to deal with, something big.

He had a son.

Had Billy been a good dad? Had he taken his anger out on Lanford's son?

"How is…Riordan?"

He broke into the conversation between the two women. Right now, he was less worried about the fire and proving his innocence. He was more worried about his son.

Allison looked startled.

"He's fine. Moody, sometimes, but most boys are at that age."

"Is Billy good to him?"

If he wasn't, if he hurt him… Lanford wasn't sure he had enough control for that.

Allison nodded. "I swear, if Billy wasn't, I would

have left him, somehow, done something. I was a stupid girl, and made a lot of mistakes, but I love Ri. I would never let anyone hurt him.

"Billy's proud of him. He runs track, like Dan. He's been offered a scholarship."

The pain hit Lanford again. Dan had had a scholarship, and he was gone, because of Billy. Because of what Lanford had done to Billy.

Allison might have made her peace with that and been willing to live with Billy getting away with it, but Lanford couldn't.

"I hope you're telling the truth."

Lanford had sworn he wasn't going to get revenge. But when it came to his son: if Billy had hurt him? He wasn't sure he could keep that promise. Pastor Harold would need to up his prayers.

Allison broke into his thoughts.

"What are you going to do?"

She looked worried. She had every reason to.

Lanford could upset her life. A paternity test would prove he was the father, and that Allison was the boy's biological mother. It would upset the facade the family had presented to the world. It would cause scandal and gossip, and they would deserve it.

But he couldn't do that to his child, not until he was sure it wouldn't hurt him.

Eighteen years ago, Lanford hadn't been in any condition to be a good father. He'd been a kid himself. But he was an adult now. He'd learned a lot and graduated from a difficult school.

He'd thought he had no family left. Now he had a son. And he would do what was best for that son, no matter the cost to himself.

It would take him time to figure out what that best was, though.

"I'm not sure."

Allison crossed her arms over her chest. "You guys don't understand what Billy's like."

"Why don't you explain?" Sarah's voice was warm, comforting. It invited confidences.

Allison gave Sarah a hard look.

"We all know he set that fire. So I know what he's capable of if I upset him. He's been good, as long as we all behave. If I tried to leave him..."

Allison's mouth set. She swallowed. "Well, if it was for Ri, I'd try. But he's proud of his son. Still... I'm positive his parents' accident wasn't actually an accident."

Sarah's eyes widened.

"Seriously?"

Allison nodded. "But you'll never prove anything."

Sarah tilted her head. "A fire with two accidental deaths is not the same as first-degree murder."

"Who says the deaths were accidental?"

Lanford wasn't sure he could handle much more of this. He was flashing cold and then hot, as Allison spilled information.

"Why would Billy have wanted to harm Riordan or Mr. Davies?"

Allison blinked her eyes. "I'd called Dan. Confessed everything. He knew Billy... I was really confused.

"I told Billy everything before—before I knew what he could do. He hated that I'd confided in Dan. Billy couldn't have carried out his plan if Dan had been alive."

Lanford had the same out-of-body experience again. Billy had wanted to kill Dan? He'd known Dan was home when he lit that fire?

It still left Lanford as the cause of this mess, but it meant there was some evil here that wasn't part of Lanford.

It didn't make him feel less guilty; it just reshaped the guilt.

"Do you want me to take you somewhere safe?" Sarah asked Allison, and Lanford suddenly recognized how this might affect Sarah. It was very similar to the case she'd told him about, the one that sent her to Balsam Grove. The one that had caused problems for her previously.

Allison rose to her feet.

"I don't know. I don't know anything. I need some time."

Sarah rose to her feet, as well, and Lanford followed.

Sarah took a card from her purse and passed it to Allison.

"We'll give you some time. I think Lanford wants that, as well. But we'll be in touch. If you need anything, give me a call. But I can't let this go, you understand that?"

Allison stared at the card before sliding it into her pocket.

"I don't know anything," she repeated.

Chapter Eighteen

Sarah was sure that Lanford had received more than enough shocks for the day. Sarah was reeling, and she was just an observer.

Wasn't she?

When they came out the front door, Festus was tied under a tree in the yard. Ri was nowhere to be seen.

Allison stood, staring at the place where the dog was lying. She moved her head, looking up and down the street. There was no sign of her son.

Lanford's son.

Sarah shot a glance at Lanford, tracing his features and wondering if Ri had uncovered the secret of his parentage, as well. The two looked so much alike. She felt for the boy, but she couldn't help him right now, and his mother was here. If he needed someone to talk to, Allison was undoubtedly the best choice. For now.

"Call me about anything, Allison. I'll be happy to talk."

Allison nodded, but quickly retreated inside the house, reaching into her pocket, probably for her phone to call her son.

Lanford went over to Festus and untied his leash. She checked how he was doing.

"Back to Balsam Grove?"

Lanford glanced at her and then the car. He nodded.

He didn't have a lot of options. He'd lost those when Billy set the fire and framed Lanford for it.

Sarah shivered. It was one thing to know a fire had taken lives. Another to suspect it was set to take those lives.

Billy was a dangerous man.

She glanced at the house again but there was no sign of Allison.

Sarah walked to the car. She'd offered help to the woman. It was all she could do. This wasn't like last time, where she had been asked by the woman at risk to step in.

She prayed that things would work out, for everyone involved. She didn't know how it could, but she wasn't God.

She unlocked the car and slid in, switching on the AC. Lanford boosted Festus into the rear seat. He closed the door and paused. Would he rather not be with her, not after all that had happened?

She was about to offer to call a cab or drop him somewhere when he opened the passenger door and got in.

He was staring straight ahead, mind obviously elsewhere.

"How about a couple of iced coffees? Then we can head to Balsam Grove and you can take some time to process."

He turned to her and nodded. "Thank you. I don't know where to even start."

"If you want to talk, I'm here. If you want to think, I can be quiet. You have some decisions coming up, but there's a lot to consider."

Lanford nodded and then stared out the passenger's window. Sarah put the car in gear and headed for the highway.

Lanford didn't speak again, beyond thanking her for the coffee. Sarah did a lot of thinking herself.

She was glad Lanford finally knew what had happened that night. Allison was right; they might never be able to prove it. But the search was over. They'd discovered the truth.

Hadn't they?

Sarah sorted through the threads she had for this case, the motivations that Allison had revealed, the information that had been carefully suppressed. In a twisted way, it all made sense.

Would Lanford be able to rest, now that he knew the truth, even if the crime remained unsolved and a blot on his reputation? Could she prove the truth of what had happened that night?

At this date, would anyone other than Allison remember Billy's movements? Billy hadn't been interviewed because no one had mentioned seeing him at the party. Even if Allison was willing to testify, Sarah feared a good lawyer could shred her story. Plus, it would obviously be the end of her marriage, and that could be twisted to be her motive.

Most of the evidence was circumstantial. It could fit Billy or Lanford. Billy was a well-respected businessman. Lanford was the troublemaker turned prisoner.

Would it be possible to get Billy on tape, admitting to what he'd done?

A long shot.

Then, the other surprise. Riordan, the seventeen-year-old son no one knew Lanford had.

Lanford might not be able to prove he was innocent of the arson and resulting deaths. But he could definitely prove that Ri was his son. Aside from the physical resemblance, there was DNA evidence he could request.

What would Billy do when that came out? Would he be embarrassed and want nothing to do with the boy, or would he fight to keep Lanford away from him?

Would Lanford want to claim his son? She had assumed he would, but she hadn't known him that long. It might be that this attraction she felt was making her attribute virtues to him that he didn't possess.

She sighed. They were less than an hour from Balsam Grove.

"I'd wondered." Lanford broke the silence. "After, when I had nothing but time to think, I wondered if maybe she'd been pregnant. But we'd always been careful. And I figured, if she was, she'd have let me know somehow. He looks just like me."

Lanford wasn't worried about proving his innocence, it seemed. His thoughts were wrapped up in the son he'd just discovered.

"I don't know what to do. I mean, do I tell him? Does Allison? Would it be better if he never found out?"

Sarah glanced over and saw that Lanford was watching her as if she had the answers.

She didn't.

"Hey, do you want to stop and grab a bite before we get back?"

Lanford glanced behind her, where Festus was quietly snoring.

"We can find something with a patio, or a take-out place with picnic tables, then we don't have to worry about Festus. If you want to talk, maybe Balsam Grove isn't the right place to do it."

Lanford nodded. "If you don't mind. I don't know what to think, or what to do. This was nothing like I imagined."

It was nothing like what Sarah had imagined, either.

She noticed a food sign at the next exit and drove off. She'd only been in the area for six months, and she hadn't done a lot of exploring. The weather had turned into summer just recently, providing little motivation to see the sights until now.

It was more than that, though. She'd thought of her stay in Balsam Grove as marking time while she rearranged her priorities so she could resume her previous life in the city.

She wasn't sure that was going to happen anymore.

Lanford had upended things for her, in ways she'd never have predicted.

She had lost her objectivity about this case because she'd lost her objectivity about this man. That wouldn't necessarily apply to other cases. But she realized she did better work when she was invested in what she was doing.

But if Lanford's name was never cleared, any connection with him would bring up her grandfather's history in the minds of the cops she worked for. She could get her job back, but without the support of her fellow officers, would it be worth it?

Lanford had made her aware of her aloneness. Something about his stoic strength reached out to her.

He'd been dealt a more difficult hand than she had. And she admired the person he'd become. Even now, when he'd discovered that he'd been framed and his family taken from him, he wasn't focused on revenge or proving his case.

She shook her head at where her thoughts were taking her. Instead, she looked for a place they could eat.

On the outskirts of the town, off the exit, was a burger and fry truck. There were picnic tables scattered under a couple of big oaks. Perfect for Festus.

She signaled her turn and pulled into the lot.

There were a couple of other vehicles, and two of the picnic tables were occupied, but there was no one she recognized. No one gave them more than a passing glance. She opened the door and Festus was eager to get out.

Lanford stood on the other side of the car.

"What would you like?"

She shook her head. "I can get—"

He gave her a small smile, and she answered with one of her own.

"My treat this time, Sarah. What would you like?"

"Burger and fries, and a Coke, thank you."

"You take care of your police dog there and find a seat. I'll join you with the food."

Sarah nodded, and let Festus pull her over to a nearby bush.

Lanford ordered the same as Sarah and waited patiently beside the window while the food was prepared.

He watched Sarah as she chose a table at a distance from the other diners.

He tried to make some order of his tangled thoughts. He'd spent a lot of the ride back praying. Not a sensible, organized prayer. The Bible verse said the Spirit would pray for him when he didn't have words, and this was one of those times.

He was relieved to finally learn what had happened to his family. He'd hoped that the tragedy might not have been a result of things he'd done, but he knew that had been stretching the possibilities.

But now what? Sarah could tell him if he had any chance of proving it. That had been his main goal when he got out, but now it took the back seat.

He had a son.

"Davies."

The voice came from the window of the food truck, and he moved over to get the order. There were two cans of Coke, moisture dripping down the sides, and two bags for the food, grease starting to stain the paper.

He thanked the woman and headed over to the picnic table where Festus and Sarah waited.

"You should give Allison a couple of days to figure things out."

He'd asked Sarah for her advice. Somehow, despite the fact that he was the ex-con and she was the sheriff, she'd become the person he was closest to in Balsam Grove. Asking her felt right.

"What do you think she'll do?"

Sarah looked away, and he knew the answer wasn't going to be what she wanted.

"It's not in her best interest to expose her husband.

You can file for a paternity test, prove that Ri is your son, but you may never prove that Billy set the fire."

Lanford gazed up into the leaves of the oak tree above them.

Maybe it wasn't necessary to prove his innocence. He'd done his time, and nothing would get those years back.

What mattered to him was that he now knew the truth, and that Sarah did, as well. He could tell Anton. But if he spread the truth to too many other people, he could easily imagine Billy suing him.

He didn't need that.

"Should I do that? Get the paternity test?"

"What do you want to do?"

Lanford brought his gaze down to the woman sitting across from him.

"I want to know my son. But more than that, I want to do what's best for him. I'm not sure that's me."

Sarah reached a hand across the table and covered his. The warmth of her palm spread up his arm, warming and relaxing his whole body.

"You're a good guy, Lanford."

Almost of its own volition, his hand turned over and gripped hers.

"You are, too, Sarah."

His cheeks warmed as he realized what he'd said.

"I mean—"

She smiled at him, letting their hands stay entwined.

"I know what you mean, and thank you. But about Riordan. You can't very well say that you're his biological father and that you never met him because his adopted father framed you for arson and two deaths.

But, as an adopted kid, he may want to know why his parents didn't raise him."

"His mother did."

Sarah frowned. "But it sounds like she never told him she was his biological mother. That could bring up some issues, as well."

"So, I should just let it go?"

Sarah shook her head. "I just wonder…what has it been like with Billy as his father?"

His stomach clenched.

"Do you think Billy…hurt him?"

"Allison says not. But Billy may have affected Ri's attitude toward life and other people.

"If Allison decides to tell the boy, then the decision is no longer yours to make. What will you do if that happens?"

"I want him to know about his grandfather and uncle. I want him to know I only just learned about him, or maybe I would have done something differently. I want him to know that loving God was what helped me straighten up.

"I want him to know I'm there if he ever needs me."

"That might make it worth talking to him." Sarah's smile was tremulous.

"Thank you." He owed Sarah so much. He never would have found out all this on his own.

Her cheeks flushed.

"So, ready to go?"

He nodded, reluctantly releasing her hand so they could gather up their garbage.

Festus decided he needed to find a bush again, but he wasn't happy with the ones nearby. He pulled Sarah down a short path at the side of the parking lot, searching for the exact right spot. Lanford followed, unwilling to let them wander off alone.

Festus was finally satisfied. It was anticlimactic, after the big revelations of the day, to be standing, watching the dog lift his leg, an expression of happiness on his canine face. Lanford heard a cardinal's call above them, and, nostalgic, glanced up to find the flash of red.

Festus, having relieved himself, headed for the car. Sarah twisted to follow, but Lanford, distracted, missed seeing them turn and was still standing there as Sarah pivoted into his chest.

He reflexively tightened his grasp around her, to keep her upright. Festus gave another tug, pulling Sarah tightly against his chest.

He was no longer looking for the cardinal. He gazed down at Sarah, whose startled face was looking up at him.

He wasn't sure he could have resisted. He kissed her.

He had no right, but he wanted to. And for once, what he wanted was right there.

She kissed him back.

That surprised him, but even though it had been years, he still remembered kissing. He raised a hand to her face, the feel of her soft skin so good.

Another tug from Festus, and Lanford had to step away to avoid falling over. Sarah raised a hand to her mouth.

Lanford thought he should apologize. But he wasn't sorry, not for kissing her. He was sorry if she was upset by it, but that kiss was the best thing he'd experienced in a long, long time.

"But I'm a cop." Was what Sarah finally said.

She didn't say he shouldn't have done it. Kissed her. But this, her job, affected if there would be another kiss.

"That means we can't..." He trailed off, wanting desperately to know what she was thinking.

"It means, why would you be interested in a cop?"

Lanford felt the smile breaking out on his face.

"I think it depends on the cop. Why would you be interested in an ex-con?"

She bit her lip.

"I guess it depends on the ex-con."

And this one, she'd heard today, hadn't committed the crime he'd served time for.

"Are you okay? I should have asked."

This time she was the one smiling, shyly. "If I wasn't okay, I'd have kneed you in the groin instead of kissing you back."

Lanford couldn't believe this was happening.

"Does this... Are we...?" He had no idea what label to put on them. What they were, what he hoped they would be, what she wanted.

"I guess it's something we need to figure out. It's been quite a day for you, Lanford Davies."

Seeing the warm look in her eyes, he leaned down, and brushed her lips one more time.

"This part? This doesn't have any downside as far as I'm concerned. This is nothing but good."

A worried expression crossed her face.

"I don't know what I'm doing, Lanford. After the next six months in Balsam Grove, I have no idea."

He shrugged. "I have no idea what I'm doing after the next six minutes."

Sarah tugged on the leash, now that Festus had given up and lain down.

"You're going to drive back to Balsam Grove with me. And we'll figure it out."

That was all the plan he needed.

Chapter Nineteen

Sarah drove them to the sheriff's office. They needed to work out their game plan, and she didn't think they should necessarily hang out at each other's places. There was a lot to consider.

There was the issue of Billy and the arson and Lanford's son, and then there was the issue of the two of them together.

Festus was happy to return to one of the places he considered home. Spending this much time with Lanford had apparently reconciled him to the man's presence, and he stretched out with a weary sigh once they'd made their way inside.

Sarah dropped her bag on her desk. She unlocked her desk drawer.

"I want to read through your case file again, see if there's anything that might support our new information."

"One moment." Lanford reached for her hand and pulled her close. His other hand touched her cheek and pushed a strand of hair behind her ear.

"May I?" he asked, eyes on her.

Sarah nodded, not sure exactly what he was asking, but she knew what she hoped.

He leaned down and pressed his lips to her. She raised to her toes, as eager as he was to build on this connection they had.

Lanford pulled away, slowly. "So, this is really a thing."

Sarah smiled. "It appears so, yes."

Lanford stepped back, releasing her hand. "I should let you do your job."

Sarah sighed. "Yes, you probably should."

She sat down in the worn seat and pulled out the file she was becoming all too familiar with.

"If you can't find anything, if we can't prove he did it, it's okay." Lanford had sat down in the seat beside her desk.

Sarah looked up at Lanford. He was staring at her intently.

"You told me, the first time I met you, that you came here to find out who had framed you and killed your family."

He nodded. "I did find out. I'd be happy if Billy paid for what he did, and I'd like to be exonerated. But the important people know the truth now. I'll never get those years back, but I can move forward."

"You aren't angry? You have every right to be."

Just thinking about it made Sarah furious, and had required a few prayers to keep the lid on her temper.

He glanced away for a moment.

"Yeah, I'm angry. I lost my family. But other things—I was on a bad path. And if I'd tried to be a dad? I have no idea how I would have done.

"Somehow, I just have to believe God is doing some

good through what's happened. And I remind myself, a lot, that the Bible says vengeance is for God alone."

Sarah was impressed. It was easy to voice the platitudes when it cost nothing, but right now, Lanford was living the hard stuff and still following through.

"Well, maybe I can help that vengeance along."

That's when the door to the station slammed open.

Sarah had to repeat the events that followed over and over again. They became part of the case file, and she had to testify in court. Lanford had to do the same. The details were carved into her memory bank.

She looked up when she heard the door. She was surprised to see Billy Robertson, bursting in with wide eyes and gritted jaw. She was equally surprised to find Ri, the boy she'd met for the first time mere hours ago behind him.

She was horrified when she realized Billy was holding a gun. And it was pointed directly at her and Lanford.

She rose to her feet and, from the corner of her eye, noticed Lanford do the same. Billy pulled back the safety on the gun and she froze.

"Lock the door, Ri, and make sure the shade is down."

At this time of year, approaching the summer solstice, the sun was still high enough in the sky that she hadn't switched on any lights. With the shade drawn, no one would spot them in here. Not even silhouettes.

Sarah knew this was going to be bad. She sent up a quick prayer.

Billy's expression was both excited and furious. There was also satisfaction in it. At that moment, Sarah had no doubt that he'd set the fire eighteen years ago, and that he'd arranged for the accident that killed his parents.

He looked like a murderer.

Ri locked the door behind his father. He pulled down the blind. No one had passed by the station in the moments between Billy's command and Ri's response. Who would they call anyway?

Sarah refused to let her eyes drop to her desk drawer, where she'd left her own weapon. She wasn't sure if she'd be able to reach it, but she wasn't going to telegraph its location to Billy.

Most days, she was in her uniform and had the weapon on her hip. Today, she was in civvies.

She was going to have to rely on her wits.

"Step away from the desk, both of you. Together now, no splitting apart. I'm not sure who I'd prefer to shoot first."

Sarah needed time. She decided to lead with ignorance.

"What are you doing, Billy—Bill? Why are you here with a gun?"

Allison must have spilled everything to him as soon as they left. Sarah hadn't thought Allison would do that—she'd appeared to be considering separating from Billy. Sarah didn't understand why he'd brought Ri, but she did know this was going to be bad if she couldn't either defuse the situation or get Billy away from his gun.

"Nice try, Sheriff. I'm sure my wife told you the whole, sad story. But she'll keep her mouth shut now."

Sarah glanced at Billy's hands, wrapped around the gun. There were no marks on his knuckles. Did that mean he hadn't physically hurt Allison? Or had he used the weapon in his hands?

Sarah frowned. Or was he implying Allison wasn't his source of information?

"She's an idiot. But my son was smart enough to come to me with what was going on."

From the corner of her eye, she noticed Lanford turn toward the boy.

"Stay still!"

Sarah willed Lanford to obey. Billy was on edge, and he had nothing to lose at this point.

"It was a bit of a shock for him to see you, Lan. He looks just like you, doesn't he?"

No one spoke.

"Yeah, a real shock for a young man to come face-to-face with his father. His biological father. The convict. This is why we didn't tell you, Ri. Your father, a murderer, and your mother, well, calling her a liar and a cheat would just be the start."

Sarah allowed her gaze to flicker to where Ri was standing behind his father. The boy looked shell-shocked. She could only imagine.

He'd obviously figured out who Lanford was. And unfortunately, he'd gone to Billy to get answers.

Billy noticed the movement of her eyes.

"Yes, Ri wasn't stupid. He waited around, heard what you were talking about and then he called his dad. He thought I didn't know all this."

Sarah somehow had to get control of the situation.

"Then he didn't listen to everything we said. He missed some vital information. He didn't hear Allison admit that you set it all up, that you lit the fire that killed Ri's uncle and grandfather, framed Lanford and then forced Allison to keep quiet."

She hoped Ri was hearing what she was saying. That the words weren't going through his head without any comprehension.

"Is that what Allison told you? It's her word against mine."

"Maybe Riordan would appreciate knowing the truth."

Billy's voice cracked with anger. "I'd appreciate you shutting your stupid mouth. It doesn't matter. After tonight, the truth will be what I say it is.

"Step away from your desk, Sheriff. Nice and slow. You and Lan, just move over there together. I've decided I'm shooting Lan first, Sheriff, so if you make a move, he's dead. I've practiced. Won some shooting awards. I won't miss at this range."

Sarah would have liked to challenge him, but he was too confident with his gun. And he looked too eager to shoot someone.

"Ri, check the desk for her handcuffs. She's sure to have some."

Ri still looked shell-shocked. He resembled the boy Lanford had been when he'd been booked for arson and third-degree murder at about the same age. Her chest tightened. This was going to scar the kid, no matter how it ended.

He'd had seventeen years of listening to Billy. He did what Billy told him. He came to her desk and started to pull open the drawers.

Sarah kept her face blank, her gaze on Billy. She knew what Ri would find.

"The handcuffs are here. And…a gun." He sounded

much more surprised than he should, considering it was a sheriff's office.

Billy smiled. "Good work, Ri. Just what we wanted. Pick up the gun and the cuffs and bring them to me."

Sarah was almost shaking with the urge to do something. But Billy had his gun pointed right at Lanford, and she had no doubts that he'd be happy for any excuse to shoot him.

She understood what had triggered the hatred, but the intensity of it wasn't quite sane.

She continued to pray.

"Is it loaded?"

Billy must have taught Ri about guns, because he checked the gun competently.

"It is."

She normally unloaded it at the end of each day. She'd been distracted.

She was sure it wouldn't have changed anything if she had taken the ammunition out. There was more in the drawer, and these two were obviously familiar with guns and could load one if necessary.

"Okay, make sure the safety's on and slip it into my pocket. We don't want these two to get their hands on it, now, do we?"

Ri slid the gun into Billy's pocket.

"You have the cuffs?"

Ri nodded. He didn't say much. Sarah wondered if that was normal for him, like Lanford, or if it was just the circumstances. It was quite possible she'd never find out.

"Sheriff, put your hands behind your back. Cuff her, Ri."

"Riordan, you don't have to—" Sarah started.

"Shut up!" Billy roared, his gaze moving from Lanford for a moment. "If I pull the trigger, that will shut you up, you stupid woman."

He looked more than ready to do so. Sarah wondered what was restraining him.

If he shot Lanford with the gun, the sound would bring people. But by then, he could also shoot her. He must plan to. There was no way she was going to lie about what was happening here. He'd have to kill her.

She had no idea what story he'd come up with to cover himself, but she was sure he had something planned.

She'd hoped, especially for Lanford's sake, that the boy wouldn't be part of this. But he was following Billy's orders like an automaton.

She hated to think what would make him do that.

She put her hands behind her back, and Ri snapped the cuffs around her wrists. She felt more helpless than before, though she hadn't been able to do anything then, either.

"Good, Ri. Good."

Billy sidled closer to where Sarah and Ri were standing. If he got close enough for her to knock into him… He was clever, though, and stayed just out of her reach.

"Ri, take the gun out of my pocket now."

Sarah almost groaned when Ri did as he was told.

"I can see the sheriff here is very curious about what's going to happen. She won't be around to understand, but I'll be magnanimous and give her the story.

"Lan just can't help himself. He's bad, through and through. The two of you were here, in the sheriff's station… Hmmm. Maybe you picked him up for something. He must be on probation, so having this weapon on him might have been why you had to bring him in. But he doesn't want to go back to prison. Do you, Lan?

"Lan, criminal that he is, shoots the sheriff with this gun." Billy waved the one in his hand. "It's had the serial numbers filed off, and no one will be able to trace where it came from. Naughty, naughty, Lanford."

Billy's smile wasn't sane.

"Well, of course the sheriff defends herself. Unfortunately, they both die. Ri and I had come down to warn her about him, but we arrived just in time for the shots."

Sarah's brain worked through the scenario. She could see the holes that he hadn't covered, but it wasn't worth telling him. It wouldn't change what he did, and if she was going to be dead, she wanted the evidence to lead to the true perpetrator.

"Ri, take these gloves. We don't want residue on our hands. We can get the fingerprints figured out when they're dead."

Ri had frozen, staring at Billy.

Billy gave Ri an impatient glance before returning his focus to Lanford.

"Come on, now, son. Today you're going to become a man. This convict, the one who looks just like you, is going to ruin all our lives. You need to protect yourself, protect your family. A man does the hard things."

Ri was still holding Sarah's gun, but his hands were shaking. Sarah watched the two of them carefully, waiting for her chance. She'd get only one opportunity before Billy started to shoot. Unlike Ri, his hand was steady, and he was prepared.

Billy was too far away from her for her to get to him. She had no chance to change the aim he had, directly at Lanford's chest.

Ri was closer. She could throw herself at him, knock the two of them to the floor. That might distract Billy enough that Lanford could move and stay alive.

She tensed, waiting for the right moment.

"Ri, this is your chance. Just raise the gun, aim it right where I have and pull the trigger. It's easy.

"It was a lot more difficult to set that fire. I hadn't had time to do any research. I took the gas can, poured it around the couch where this guy was passed out, drunk—"

The fury was rolling off Billy, but his hand stayed steady.

"I thought Dan and his dad might get out, but I wasn't worried about them, not then. But everything worked out for the best. I didn't need Dan shooting off his mouth about your mother.

"I couldn't believe it when Lan staggered out of the house. But then he fell over and knocked himself out.

"I didn't have time to pull him back into the house since the sirens were getting close, but I managed to wipe off my fingerprints and put his hand on the gas can instead."

Billy shook his head at Lanford.

"You should have died. You were supposed to die. And now you will."

Billy spared another glance for Ri, but the boy was still frozen.

"Ri, you can do this. It's what we Robertsons do." Billy laughed, almost a giggle. "I had time to do some research for the crash that took care of my dad. I did an excellent job. Everyone thought it was an accident.

"Only a man can pull that trigger, Ri. I know you can do it. Show me you're a man."

Ri dropped his gaze to the gun. His whole body began to tremble.

Billy sighed.

"Come on, Ri, I can help you."

Billy moved over to the boy, gaze flickering between Lanford and Ri. Sarah tensed, waiting for her moment, hoping it was going to work.

Then, things went crazy.

Lanford could do nothing but pray.

Billy had everything prepared, everything ready to kill him. Lanford knew Sarah would try to do something. She was a cop. This is what she was trained for.

He didn't know what God had planned for him. This afternoon, when he'd kissed Sarah, he'd experienced a happiness he hadn't known since long before the fire.

Maybe that was his last blessing, before his life down here was over. If so, he'd be grateful for it.

He felt a strange peace—until Billy gave Ri the gun.

He knew Billy was evil. He wasn't sure why, but he suspected his dad had done something to twist him. But *his* son, Ri, wasn't there yet. He didn't want Billy to twist up Ri the way Billy's father had done to Billy.

Lanford had made a lot of mistakes by the time he was Ri's age. He'd paid for them. He didn't want that for his son, the boy he'd only learned about hours ago.

He was reconciled to the idea of his own life ending, but he didn't want to mess up Ri's life.

With Billy's gun pointed at him, he couldn't do much. But he could pray.

He didn't look at Billy. He looked at Ri. He saw the panic in the boy's eyes. He wanted to urge him not to do it, but he didn't know how to tell him in a way that wouldn't make Billy start shooting at Sarah, as well.

He prayed. It was all he could do. But he had confidence God could intervene.

Billy moved toward Ri. Sarah tensed, ready to try some desperate measure to save the situation.

And then, Billy tripped on Festus.

Lanford had forgotten about the dog. He hid every time someone came in the room, and that had happened when Billy entered, as well. This time, though, he wasn't under the desk, he'd been behind it.

Billy had been focused on Lanford and Sarah. He hadn't been watching his feet. Maybe Festus had been comfortable with Ri after meeting him this afternoon, or maybe Ri had walked around him. But Billy wasn't watching where he stepped, and he stepped right into Festus.

It knocked Billy off-balance, tilting him sideways. Festus jumped to his feet after getting Billy's shoe in his ribs, and he crossed into Billy's path again. Billy tumbled to the ground, swearing, but he kept his grip on his gun.

He landed on the floor, his head next to Sarah. She kicked his temple with all she had. She lost her balance after her foot connected, falling over. She landed, without her cuffed hands to break her fall, sprawled awkwardly on Billy. Billy didn't get up.

Billy's face was slack, his eyes closed. The gun skittered across the floor, out of Billy's grasp.

Lanford swung his gaze back to Ri. The boy had raised the gun, holding it up toward Lanford. It trembled in his hands, but the boy was panicked. He could pull the trigger reflexively, and it was aimed right at Lanford's head.

Lanford was confident that Sarah, squirming on the floor, would make sure Billy didn't get his hands on the loose gun. But right now, his son was scared, ready to do anything.

Lanford couldn't let him pull the trigger. Couldn't let the boy find himself a murderer, not at seventeen.

Lanford had been there, and he wanted to save his son.

"Riordan, don't do this. Billy was wrong. This is wrong. There's no way you can get away with this."

Lanford heard sounds, knew Sarah was trying to get the gun from the floor. She couldn't stop Ri, though. Lanford wasn't sure anything would get through to him, not while he stood there, pupils blown wide, shocked and panicked.

"Riordan, I messed up my life when I was seventeen. I did a lot of things I regret and hurt a lot of people. It ended up costing me my family.

"I can tell you, it's a horrible thing to live, knowing you did something like that. It shadows the rest of your life and makes it worse. You don't want to do what I did."

The gun was still shaking, but Ri's knuckles were white. Lanford wasn't sure he could reach him.

He could accept that. But he didn't want his son to suffer.

"I don't think you should do this, but if you do, know that I forgive you. I can't imagine what all has happened to you, but you're my son, and I don't want to put a burden on you. God forgave me for the things I did, and He'll forgive you, too."

Lanford closed his eyes. He didn't want to see the moment that his son decided to pull the trigger. He prayed for Ri, and for Sarah, and waited for the end.

And waited. Then he heard a loud crash. He opened his eyes. The gun was on the ground in front of Ri. The boy's face crumpled as he started to cry.

Lanford didn't remember moving, but he found his arms wrapped around his son, holding the shaking figure.

"It's okay." He felt the tremors racking the boy's body. "It's okay. We'll fix everything. It's gonna be okay."

"Lanford?"

Sarah was on the ground beside him, arms still cuffed behind her.

"I'm relieved that things worked out, more than I can say, but if you could get me loose before Billy comes to…"

Chapter Twenty

It took a long time to get the paperwork done.

Sarah had called in the state police. After Lanford had released her, she'd used the cuffs to restrain Billy and dumped him in her holding cell until he came to. When he woke up, it was clear he'd tipped over the border from crazed but functional to deluded, raining down threats on her and Lanford and his wife and Riordan.

She'd shut the door.

Ri had pulled away from Lanford, once his emotions had calmed down. He was embarrassed by his breakdown, mortified that he'd called his father after overhearing their discussion with his mother and horrified at what Billy had tried to do.

Sarah had given him a soda from the fridge and let him settle on a chair in the corner.

Lanford was also in a state of shock, so she'd pressed a soda into his hand, as well. He'd opened his mouth to speak, but Sarah had stopped him.

"I have to be able to say that we haven't discussed this. We haven't collaborated on our stories."

Lanford had watched her for a moment, then nodded. He took a chair next to Ri, not speaking, but being close in case he was needed.

Sarah called Allison. It was a relief to hear that Billy hadn't spoken to her. He must have met Riordan somewhere and come straight to Balsam Grove.

Then the state troopers arrived, and the familiar, tedious process began.

It could have been much worse. Sarah was a cop, and that gave her the presumption of truth with the other officers. She appreciated that privilege.

Allison arrived and sat in on the interrogations with her son. Sarah was careful to inform the other law officers that Lanford, while an ex-con, had been sentenced for a crime Billy had just admitted to.

It wasn't a lot to throw against the clout Billy carried as a wealthy member of society, but Billy had lost his calm, and was now vacillating between screaming out all the repercussions he'd rain down on the police officers holding and interrogating him and bragging about how clever he was and that they'd never prove anything against him.

Lawyers arrived for Billy and Riordan. Pastor Harold came to support Lanford, and at some point, they must have been allowed to leave, because when Sarah looked up, they were gone.

Sarah wasn't sure if Lanford had left without speaking to her to be diplomatic, or because she'd told him they shouldn't talk, or if the tenuous connection they'd experienced couldn't withstand what had just happened.

She didn't have the luxury of choice. She had to focus on making sure the truth came out.

It was very late when she finally escaped to her own home. Her station was still full of cops, all working to gather evidence, organize information and file their reports.

They told her they'd let her know when she could return to work. There was no indication that she was in any trouble; she'd never drawn her gun, and it was obvious that the one act of violence she'd committed, kicking Billy, had been in self-defense.

It was incredible that after all that Billy had planned, the only violence had come from a trip over a dog and a kick from her sandaled foot.

She slept late the next day, exhausted physically and mentally.

She'd turned off all the notifications on her phone, and left it charging on her bedside table, not yet ready to face what had happened. Her head was groggy from the unfamiliar sleep pattern, and she took her cup of coffee out to her tiny deck to wake her brain cells.

"Lots of excitement last night!"

Arthur's head popped over the fence, his own excitement visible in his expression.

The grapevine had obviously been going full throttle.

"It was something, all right." Sarah was careful not to confirm anything until she was notified she could do so safely.

"I feel bad that I never questioned whether Lanford had set that fire." Arthur was shaking his head.

Sarah wondered where his information had come from. She'd only spoken to the cops, and it was hard to imagine Lanford spilling his guts, or even Pastor Harold.

She'd heard about small-town gossip, but this was more than she would have imagined.

"I can't say anything until the investigation is complete."

Arthur's bushy eyebrows rose.

"It's online. Everyone knows."

Sarah was shocked. Arthur chuckled.

"Maybe you want to go see what's out there. But, good work, Sheriff. You've changed Lanford's life."

Sarah promptly returned to the house, reaching for her phone.

Several articles had already been published, and they had more information than she did. She supposed, as a witness, she'd been kept out of the loop, and it didn't feel good.

The journalists didn't reveal their sources, but Sarah suspected Allison.

Billy had been submitted for a psych evaluation. He'd bragged of what he'd done, both the fire and his parents' car accident.

Lanford was mentioned. They reported that he'd been sentenced for the deaths in the arson case, and recently been released.

They described Sarah as the key investigator on this cold case.

Then she finally faced the missed notifications on her phone.

Calls to the station had been forwarded to her cell phone and her voice mail was full. Texts were coming in from old friends and colleagues and media outlets.

The story had caught the attention of the public, and Sarah could see that it was going to take a while to settle down.

She wondered how Lanford was dealing with things, and if the media had located him at the parsonage.

If he needed her, how would she know? He didn't even have a phone, and she didn't dare go to him.

She swallowed.

Sarah desperately wanted to see Lanford, but she was afraid to compromise the case. Their relationship, such as it was, was so new. If this went to trial, their romantic connection could be used in Billy's defense. Lanford deserved to be exonerated. He deserved a second chance at a good life. She would have to be patient.

And pray. Somehow, that occurred to her as a last resort, but she knew it was her best choice.

And she needed the time to consider her own future. Would this look like she was siding with criminals? Or would it be seen as good detective work by her peers?

She'd come to this town to evaluate her priorities. This case with Lanford had strengthened her belief that her values had been correct all along.

That might mean she couldn't return to her job in Pittsburgh. She didn't know if her father would understand.

Just like with her relationship with Lanford, she'd have to pray and trust God would show her the right path.

If God was behind this thing between her and Lanford, it would last. And the rest would work out. Maybe not the way she'd thought or planned, but she would trust it would all be right.

A week later, things were finally settling down.

The media circus had quieted, distracted by a political scandal. Sarah had her station to herself. Everyone in town had talked to her about the case, and she had finally gone for coffee without getting the third degree.

She'd also heard from Ron Harding's wife. He was in a home, suffering from dementia.

Sarah would never find out if Festus had any skills.

She still hadn't seen Lanford. She didn't know what he'd been told or how he was feeling about all the changes that had happened. She'd decided to give him some time.

But now Sarah was tired of waiting. She'd heard from the state police that Lanford would be exonerated. But she needed to know how he felt about her. She was going to find him.

She swung by the church, but there was no tall figure working on the grounds. She parked and walked into the building, searching for Lanford. She found Pastor Harold.

"Sheriff! Lots of excitement around town. I'm so happy no one was hurt or killed. I've been praying for that unfortunate man, Billy Robertson. I cannot understand how a person could be convinced to do something so…heinous."

Sarah hadn't been praying much for Billy but acknowledged she probably should have.

"How is Lanford? Is he around?"

Pastor Harold sighed. "I've been praying for him, as well. It's a lot to handle, and he's done well. I feared he would succumb to anger, but he has a very balanced view. We've chatted. There were some media types around the church, so he was working inside, rather than out. He mowed the lawns first thing in the morning to avoid the press."

"Is he here?"

Pastor Harold shook his head.

"He went out for a walk. I can tell him you're looking

for him. He should buy a phone. Perhaps now… Well, I've heard there was a fund, raising money for him. He hasn't wanted to touch it yet, but there's time for him to figure out what he wants to do with himself."

Sarah thanked Pastor Harold and returned to her car.

She'd spent the previous day at the station getting caught up on what she'd missed while the case was being settled. Fortunately, the excitement, and perhaps the presence of so many police officers had kept the local rule breakers quiet.

She'd had a phone call, from the department in Pittsburgh. It had been a surprise, but a pleasant one. She had an option for her future, as far as her career went.

But she wanted to talk to Lanford before she made any decisions.

She pulled the car into gear and drove out to the U-Stor. It was the only place she could imagine where Lanford might be.

He was.

Lanford was standing, hands in his pockets, staring at the storage facility that Billy had built on his family's land. According to Allison, Billy had wanted to remove all traces of Lanford and his family. Allison thought he'd been afraid he'd left some kind of clue behind, as well.

The results were the same.

There was a new sign up, indicating that there were some legal issues, and a phone number to call for information. The place was closed. Since Lanford hadn't lit the fire, the place should be his. It was a legal fiasco. A lawyer for the wrongfully convicted had reached out to him, and he was grateful for the help.

He heard a car drive up behind him.

This place hadn't been busy before. He didn't expect anyone to be here this morning looking to put their extra possessions in a locker, even if things were normal.

He heard a door open, and footsteps. Then another door and the scrabble of paws.

It was Sarah. He sent up a quick prayer. He wasn't sure what was going to happen to his life now. He hoped Sarah was a part of it.

He'd given her space to do her job. He didn't want to pressure her. He especially didn't want to hear her say their kisses had been a mistake, so he'd been content to wait.

He'd learned patience in prison.

Festus came and sat at his feet. He felt a smile lift his mouth. Festus had grown on him, especially after his help with Billy. Perhaps he'd grown on Festus, as well.

He felt Sarah's presence when she walked to stand beside him. If he looked at her, what expression would he find on her face? Could he bear it if it was discomfort?

"I hear they're processing a pardon for you."

He nodded. Her voice was noncommittal, not revealing anything.

"It will take time, but this place will come to you. Have you made any plans for it?"

He shook his head. "It's not my home now. Even if nothing had been built here, with Dad and Dan gone, it wouldn't be my home."

He didn't want or need this place. It had good and bad memories, but it wasn't part of his life now. Now that he'd found justice, found the truth of what had happened that night, it was a load lifted from his shoulders.

"What about Riordan and Allison?"

He drew in a breath.

"We're going to counseling, the three of us. Work some things out. Allison still has some legal issues, but she's living at their home with Riordan. He and I are going to spend some time together. See how to be family."

"That's good, right?"

He nodded. "It is. I want to share my family with him. All I have is words, though." He wanted to tell Ri about Dan and his dad. Thanks to the fire, though, he had nothing but memories.

"Actually, you might have more than that. My neighbor told me he's reached out to an old friend of his who used to work on the local paper. Arthur, like a lot of people in town, feels badly about misjudging you. They're going to see if there are any photos of Dan or your parents that they can dig up in the old newspaper files."

It was more than he could have asked for. This, right now, all that had happened, was more than he'd imagined when he arrived in Balsam Grove.

He was free. Much more than he had been when the prison doors had opened to let him walk out.

"'The truth shall make you free.'" He quoted the verse and felt the meaning of it more directly than he ever had before.

"Are you free now, Lanford?"

There was hesitation in Sarah's voice. He turned to her.

Her features were still, but her eyes asked questions. Not just if he was free, but more. How he was, and what he thought, now that it was all over.

"I am. Free. And I don't really know what to do with myself."

He'd had a mission, after he finished his sentence. That mission was complete. He hadn't made plans after that.

She nodded. "You'll have money coming, eventually. Without a prison record, there will be a lot of opportunities out there for you."

"I think, for now, I'm going to keep on as I am. Pastor Harold says I can stay at the church. There's a lot of stuff I need to consider before I make a decision."

"That sounds like a wise plan. Is there anything I can do to help?"

Lanford felt his pulse pick up. He understood what she was asking. It wasn't about his job, but about the two of them. If there was going to be a two of them.

He needed to be brave, and relationships weren't something he had a lot of experience with. But more important than what he decided, or where he ended up now, was knowing who he would end up with.

"You could tell me if I can make plans with you."

His cheeks heated. It was easier to face the people in town who'd believed him an arsonist and murderer than it was to meet Sarah's gaze right now.

"Do you want to?"

Sarah looked as uncomfortable as he was. He held her gaze, though, and nodded.

A smile broke across her face, and he felt lighter. "I do, too."

He took a long breath. "Well, you're here, in Balsam Grove, for the next while, right?"

Sarah nodded.

"I'm sure I can stay at the church for the same length of time."

Sarah tilted her head. "I got a phone call from the department in Pittsburgh."

He focused on her expression. It was hesitant, but not fearful, and not upset.

"Good news? They want you to return?"

She nodded. "But not in the same capacity."

He waited. Knowing that they were making plans together was enough to keep a buoyant feeling of happiness inside, something he hadn't experienced for years. Decades.

"This, your case, is what we'd consider a cold case. Something old, ignored, not solvable at the time.

"Your case had been solved, but incorrectly. There are a lot of old cases, ones that haven't had any solution. They'd like me to work on those."

"Is that what you want?"

Sarah bit her lip. "I believe so. I can focus on each one, and not have to worry about politics and current cases—I think I would like it."

"Then you should take the job."

Her teeth were still worrying her lip.

"And you…"

He reached over, took her hand and laced their fingers together.

"You said there would be lots of opportunities for me. I can look for those in Pittsburgh. Maybe I can take up that offer of driving a truck. Like my dad did."

Relief washed over Sarah's face.

"I still have to finish my contract here. We'll work it out."

"Together."

Sarah wrapped an arm around his waist, and nothing had ever felt so good.

He dropped his forehead to hers. “Together.”

A heavy weight dropped across his feet. He looked down and saw Festus stretched over both their shoes.

“We’ll have to take Festus with us,” Sarah said, a ghost of a giggle in her voice.

“As you wish. But for now…”

He reached down and pressed his lips to hers. And let gratitude take root in his soul.

* * * * *

After the cold case murder investigation of Cassie Wheeler's husband suddenly reignites, the bounty hunter is determined to jump into the middle of it. But someone is willing to use deadly force to stop the investigation...

Read on for a sneak peek at
Cold Case Manhunt *by Jenna Night*
available August 2021 from Love Inspired Suspense.

"What do you want with me?" Cassie demanded of the masked man pointing a gun at her.

"Shut up!" he snapped, shoving her toward the open door of the van.

This *had* to be about Jake's murder. The attacks had started after she'd gotten that lead on a possible witness. At this point it seemed too much to believe that the timing of these attacks was simply coincidental.

"Where are you taking me?"

They hadn't said much to her or to each other in front of her, and now she wanted to get them talking. Maybe something would give her a hint about who they were or where they were from.

"Move!" The thug shoved his gun into her side.

If she got into that van, she'd never get out alive. *Lord, give me strength and guidance.* If only she hadn't left her weapon in the safe back at the bail bonds office.

LICCEXP0821

"If you take a shot at me, my bounty hunters will be on you in a heartbeat," she declared boldly, even as icy fear tightened its grip and she felt herself beginning to tremble. "I'm sure they're already looking for me."

Her phone was on vibrate mode and she'd felt it going off several times now. Someone was trying hard to get ahold of her. Probably Leon.

"You're not going to get away with this."

The closest gunman glanced at his partner.

That was when Cassie tried to twist her upper body out of his grip while kicking at him.

Both thugs immediately grabbed her arms. Their grips were painfully tight.

She lifted her feet off the ground, hoping that the sudden weight of her body would throw them off balance, give her a chance to escape. But it didn't work.

One of the abductors kept a hand on her arm while he tucked away his gun, then he wrapped his free hand around her neck. The other shoved his gun into his waistband and reached for Cassie's feet.

She kicked and thrashed as hard as she could. She screamed, louder than she'd ever screamed in her life. Instantly, she felt a viselike pressure on her throat followed by a sudden sharp pain to the side of her head.

And then everything went dark.

SPECIAL EXCERPT FROM

LOVE INSPIRED

INSPIRATIONAL ROMANCE

MOUNTAIN RESCUE

Will Morgan brought his teenage daughter to the Smoky Mountains to reconnect while on a rafting trip. But when disaster strikes, he and photographer Taylor Holt will have to survive the mountain wilderness to find her...

Read on for a sneak peek at Smoky Mountain Danger *by April Arrington, available September 28, 2021.*

"Ain't nothing like pushing through one last set of chaos before resting peaceful under the stars."

Taylor smiled. Jax's easygoing nature and good sense of humor made it hard not to like him. He looked to be in his early sixties and had a deep appreciation for nature.

"It's the chaos part that bothers me," Will said. "This is the roughest stretch of water I've seen in a while. We'd do better to hike back upriver and—"

"No way." Andi glared at Will. "Why'd you go through with this if all you planned to do was drag me back home the second day?"

Will frowned. "I'm just watching out for you."

"You don't think I can pull it off." Eyes glistening, Andi started walking back down the overlook. "I should never have come out here with you."

LIMREXP0821

"Andi!" A muscle ticked in Will's jaw as he called after his daughter, then smiled tightly at Taylor. "Sorry about that. She's…"

Hurt. Afraid. Aching for attention. Taylor shook her head. "It's okay. I didn't mean to encourage her."

But you did. Will didn't say the words, but the accusation in his dark gaze screamed the sentiment.

"You brought her to the right place, Will." Jax clamped his hand on Will's shoulder. "Those rough waters are good at pushing people closer together. Closer to God, too."

Taylor stared at the raging river.

"Know what my ol' pops used to say?" At Will's silence, Jax continued. "Used to say, when the world broke a man, all he had to do was come to God's land and let Him know he's here. Peace is in this place—all around. You just got to look for it."

Will moved out of Jax's grip and faced them. "In the past, I always ran a river first before bringing Andi with me. That way I'd know what I was getting her into." Will stared at the rapids, remaining silent, then headed back down the steep, rocky bank. "I'll check with Beth and Martin," he said over his shoulder. "See what they want to do. If they're gung ho on tackling the rapids, I'll agree to it—but only if the majority of the group votes to proceed."

Jax frowned as they watched Will walk away and then said, "Pray we make it through those rapids in one piece. If anything happens to Andi, Will's gonna come after us both."